SINdicate

BT Urruela FanFiction
Cerberus MC Book 1.5
BY: Marie James

Copyright

SINdicate
Copyright © 2016 Marie James
Editing by Mr. Marie James & Hale's Harem Betas ;)
Cover design by Kari Ayasha of Cover to Cover Designs
EBooks are not transferrable. All rights are reserved. No part of this book may be used or reproduced in any manner without written permission, except in the case of brief quotations embodied in critical articles and reviews. The unauthorized reproduction or distribution of this copyrighted work is illegal. No part of this book may be scanned, uploaded, or distributed via the Internet or any other means, electronic or print, without the publisher's permission.
This book is a work of fiction. The names, characters, places, and incidents are products of the writer's imagination or have been used fictitiously and are not to be construed as real. Any resemblance to persons, living or dead, actual events, locale, or organizations is entirely coincidental.

Chapter 1
BT

The stinging slap across my face echoes off of the walls in the silent room. Aviana gasps and pulls her hands to her mouth as her eyes widen in shock. I can't help but smirk when I feel the heat of her handprint spread across my face.

"Out of all of the things you could've done, you think hitting me is your best course of action?" I attempt animosity and the deepest growly voice I can manage in this situation.

I take a step toward her, and she takes a step back.

"BT!" The teacher says from across the room. "I know she's adorable, but you have to wipe that shit-eating grin off of your face if you're going to convince the audience that you're pissed that you've been smacked." She sighs and shakes her head.

I turn my head to the teacher and shrug my shoulders. "I'll work on it."

The teacher winks at me as if she knows something I don't.

"Sorry," I hear Aviana mutter from beside me. I tilt my head at her in confusion. "I didn't mean to hit you that hard."

I huff playfully. "I've been hit harder before."

"That's all for today class," the teacher announces as she makes her way across the room to Aviana and me. "I'd tell you guys to pick different partners, but we start work on kissing scenes tomorrow." She cuts her eyes between us. "I have a gut feeling you guys will get *that* right."

I follow the teacher with my eyes as she exits the class with the other students. When I cut my gaze back to the petite blonde that has had my attention for weeks, I notice the look of shock on her face. She cuts her eyes away from mine and crosses the room to gather her things. *Is she still shocked at hitting me or at what the teacher just said?*

Like a lost puppy, I follow. My jacket is in the chair right beside her purse and a few books.

"Hey," I say grabbing her attention again. "I was wondering if you wanted to hang out this evening."

She remains silent as she busies herself by stacking and restacking her books. Just as I'm beginning to wonder if she's ignoring me or didn't hear me at all, she responds.

"What did you have in mind?" She clutches her stack of books to her chest. My pulse gains speed. She's blown me off time and time again, but she's never once seemed to entertain the idea of hanging out.

"Figured you could come over. I can make dinner," I shrug trying to remain as nonchalant as possible. "Watch a movie?"

She grins at me but then narrows her eyes. "Did you just ask me over for Netflix and Chill?"

I throw my head back and laugh. By the time I'm able to calm myself enough to look back at her, I see a small smile playing on her lips. "I have Blu-ray also."

The composure she's trying to maintain fails and her smile widens. "Is that so?"

I nod my head. "I make a mean spaghetti," I entice her.

She shifts her weight and reaches to move her purse strap back on her shoulder, just for it to fall down to the crook of her elbow again.

I reach up and rub my face, certain that the handprint she left is gone by now. "You owe me for the assault," I say, trying to gain sympathy.

"That's not how it works," she says, not buying into my bullshit.

"That's how it should be," I tell her, dropping my hand from my cheek.

I widen my smile, certain that pouting at this point wouldn't work.

"You're quite the charmer; you know that?"

I'm captivated by the way the light reflects off of the brown flecks in her hazel eyes. If I didn't mistakenly leave my man card on the dresser at home, no doubt I'd have to pull it from my wallet and hand it over to her.

"We can watch *The Office*," I finally say when her blink breaks the spell she's wielding over me. "Consider it homework for acting class."

She raises an eyebrow at me suspiciously. "You realize you've asked me out over a dozen times? What makes you think today is going to be any different?"

"I figure my luck has to change eventually."

The way her eyes dart to my mouth as I speak, causing her to lick her own lips makes me hopeful.

"Dinner and a movie, huh?"

I nod.

"I do love spaghetti." She taps her finger against her lips, contemplating my offer playfully.

"Salad and garlic toast also," I say to sweeten the deal.

"Well in that case, how can I resist?"

I'm like a giddy puppy as the desire to bounce around and fist pump the air barely stays hidden. Rather than embarrass myself by doing a quick celebration dance, I hold out my hand to her.

"What?" she asks looking down at my empty hand.

"I need your phone so I can add my name."

She hands it over, and I text myself from her phone and add my contact info into her favorites.

I hand it back and pull out my phone that just buzzed in my pocket. I shoot my address to her phone.

"Seven o'clock sound good?" I ask.

"Sounds perfect," she answers.

We just stand looking at each other. I want to reach out and hug her for some strange reason, but I can't determine if that would be stepping over a line she hasn't approved yet.

"Okay," she says breaking the awkwardness. "See you at seven."

She side steps me and exits the room just as another class begins to file through the door. A quick look at my watch informs me I have six hours to get groceries, hit the gym, and make sure the house is presentable.

I nod a hello at several of the guys coming into the classroom. I've been taking classes here for several months now and have made a few acquaintances. Everyone is friendly… on the outside. If anything, I've discovered that we're all technically in competition with each other. We all want the same roles. We all show up for the same castings. Most are cordial in the halls of the acting academy, but very few are interested in actual friendship.

I have tons of friends and fans for that matter. I don't have much time to add anything extra to my plate. Between acting class, work at the gym, writing, and *Warrior Inc.* I have hardly a free minute to myself. That being said, I'll rearrange whatever I need to if it means I can spend time with Aviana Maguire outside the walls of this school.

I've been flirting with her for weeks, since this block of classes began. She's absolutely beautiful, but it's her shyness in class that drew me to her. The contradiction of wanting to be an actress in any capacity and being as shy as she seems, made me want to get to know her more.

Her shyness has helped me wiggle my way into her good graces. We partner up a lot in class to work on various skills the teacher deems mandatory of a good actor. I approached her the first day, and it seems I've made at least enough of an impression that she hasn't turned me down each time I've asked. That right there gives me hope.

I can't even think about class tomorrow. I'm excited about kissing techniques for actors and terrified all at the same time. Maybe I can persuade her into practicing some of those techniques tonight, if anything so we won't be awkward and nervous tomorrow in class.

I climb up in my truck and pull out my cell phone. After adding Aviana's name into the contacts, I shoot her a quick text, hoping she won't think I'm psycho for contacting her so soon.

BT: Do you have any food allergies/aversions?

I put the truck in drive and make my way across town to the gym. I have only one client today, so after his session and my own workout, I have nothing but time for dinner with Aviana.

I pull up to the gym, grab my bag, and my phone out of the console.

Looking at the screen, I see she has replied.

Aviana: I don't particularly like onions, but I have no allergies that I'm aware of.

I pocket my phone, making a mental list of the things I need to get from the store. I've done a lot of traveling for various photo shoots recently, so I know my fridge is practically bare. I adjust my grip on the gym bag and head to the locker room. I love my job here almost as much as I love to work out myself, but I have to admit I'm hoping the next couple of hours fly by.

Chapter 2
Aviana

I've sworn off dating and relationships for good. With my childhood and the destruction I've seen two people capable of causing each other, I'm certain there's no chance that happily ever after even exists. I know some couples *look* happy in public, but that doesn't mean things are as they seem behind closed doors.

My parents *looked* happy in public, but once they were sealed behind the thick front door of my first childhood home, they were at each other's throats constantly. The fake smiles and happy personas came out again the minute they stepped off the front porch. That was, until my mother had finally had enough.

My dad left one day when I was eleven years old and never came back. I didn't hear from him for ten years and when he finally sought me out, he hadn't changed from the memories I had of him from childhood. Many of the fights between my parents were always about money and how he was spending more than she could make. I never remember my dad having an actual job, and much of the family strife was centered on that fact.

Mom? I'd like to be able to tell you that Mom got better after Dad left, but things just kind of stayed the same. For a while, it would just be us, then she'd get a boyfriend. The boyfriends eerily reminded me of my father. They didn't work and came with their own set of issues, whether it be drugs, gambling, or both.

Due to my less than perfect upbringing, I've made sure, up until this point, to avoid anything that could possibly resemble a relationship. This is why I was beyond shocked when I said yes to BT when he asked me over earlier.

BT. Where do I even begin? He's gorgeous, a veteran, quick-witted, and the beard damn near slays me every time I look at his face, and that's only when I don't get trapped first by his magnificent brown eyes.

What's the problem then? BT screams relationship. He seems like the guy who's just waiting for his soulmate to come along. I know I'm not that person, so I never felt like it was right for me to stand in the way of him meeting her, whoever she may be.

I can't even tell you how many times he's asked me out. I've turned him down each and every time, until today. Today, the back and forth banter I've grown fond of made me, for a split second, want to be that girl. A second. A flash of urgency for him when my palm slapped his face in class. I nearly groaned when my hand met the roughness of his beard, and I tried to play it off and covered my mouth with my hands.

I should've agreed to go out with him but insisted that we head some place public, but I don't date. I'd be lying if I said I haven't noticed how sexy his arms look when they pull the fabric of his t-shirts. I'd be an idiot for not taking in the expanse of his back and the way every muscle in his body dances like a well-orchestrated symphony when he moves.

He's absolute perfection, and most people would think I'm nuts for not jumping at the many chances he's offered to hang out, but once again, I don't date. He's the talk of all the girls at the acting academy. Many have flirted with him and only received a gentlemanly rebuff to their offers; rebuffs that I hear ranged from just going on a date to some of the things I'm ashamed I've pictured doing with him myself.

Now the consensus is that he has to be gay. I know he's not for several reasons. One, he's also turned down the gay guys in the class. Two, I catch him watching me with the same look on his face that I know I must have when I'm watching him.

I caught that look more than once today. It was hungry and lustful. So I'm hoping tonight goes the way I'm thinking he wants it to, the way I want it to, which is also the only way I involve myself with a man. I said I don't date, not that I'm a prude and don't like sex. As a matter of fact, I love sex. I just haven't had any in a while; another reason I think I finally caved at his offer this afternoon.

I pinch my cheeks, attempting to add some color to my face. I'm in a loose fitting t-shirt and some cute leggings I bought online. I'm cute but not 'this is a date' cute. Plus, the leggings are super easy to get off, and they stretch in case there happens to be a little hanky-panky later.

A quick look at my watch tells me I have fifteen minutes to make the twenty-minute trek to his house. I don't want to seem overeager, even though I could easily admit I'm actually looking forward to where this evening will lead. I mean, I'll admit it to myself, just not anyone else.

Due to traffic, the trip over took even longer than I'd thought, so a simple five-minute tardiness has now turned me into a fifteen-minute late asshole. I'm an even bigger jerk for leaving my phone sitting on the bathroom counter, so when I realized just how late I was going to be I couldn't shoot off a text to him. I clear my throat, ready to apologize as I raise my hand to knock on his door. I don't hear any noise coming from inside so I push the lit doorbell to the right. I glance around the adorable neighborhood as I wait for him to answer.

Eventually, I hear rustling and his voice as he talks to someone inside. I can see now that we won't be alone, the direction I'd hoped for probably won't come to fruition tonight. I'm a little disappointed and begin to wonder if in fact he isn't actually asexual and just wants to be friends.

The door is tugged open, and I look up into his mesmerizing brown eyes. I see a wave of relief wash over his face. Seems he thought I was going to stand him up.

It's not until I hear, "Stop, Scout!" that I notice the small brown and white ball of fur circling my legs fast enough to make me dizzy.

He bends at the waist and scoops up the anxious dog, cradling it in his arms as it tries to wiggle free.

"Sorry," he apologizes. "We don't get much company. She's more of an attention whore than a guard dog."

I immediately drop my purse on the porch, take a step forward and scratch the adorable little dog's ears. She licks my hands and continues to wiggle in his grasp.

"You're such a cute little thing aren't you?" Embarrassed with the little baby voice that always seems to sneak out when I'm around adorable animals, I raise my eyes to him to find him watching. I take a step back, give the dog a final pat on the head, and pick up my purse.

"Sorry I'm late," I say holding my purse strap in both hands in front of my body.

"Don't worry. Dinner's almost ready." He turns and places the dog on the floor at his feet only for her to skitter back out on the porch and wiggle around my feet once more.

I reach down and pick her up because that's just what you do when a tiny dog wants attention.

"She sheds," he warns as he opens the door wider for me to step past him into his home.

"Most dogs do," I say with a wink as he watches me pass him.

He chuckles lightly and closes the door behind me. He holds his hand out indicating my purse and hangs it on a hook inside the entryway closet. The smell of delicious food hits my nose, and I'm certain my stomach is going to cause even further embarrassment soon when it begins to grumble.

"It smells delicious in here," I admit as he turns toward what I assume is the kitchen.

"I'm Sicilian and Cuban," he says over his shoulder. "Cooking sort of comes naturally."

I watch as he makes his way to the stove to stir the sauce that continues to taunt my empty stomach and wait for others to join us.

"Is it just us?" I probe. He gives me a smile that says *who else would be here?* "I heard you talking to someone before you opened the door." I hook my finger over my shoulder indicating where we'd just come from.

"I was talking to her," he says pointing at the dog hanging out peacefully in my arms. "I was making sure she knew to mind her manners when the pretty girl came in the house." He looks down lovingly at the almost weightless dog. "Scout doesn't listen very well."

I look down at Scout and smile, hoping he thinks it has more to do with the dog than him calling me pretty. She's licking my hands and progressing her way to my wrist.

"I think she likes the lotion I put on," I say.

He clears his throat causing me to look back up at him. "Well if you taste as good as you smell, I can see why she won't stop licking you."

He winks at me and turns back to the stove just as I feel my cheeks flush at his words; the double meaning doesn't go unnoticed, and now I'm ecstatic that we're the only ones here.

Yep, I think to myself, *definitely not gay.*

I gently place the dog on the floor and look around his almost obsessively clean kitchen as he begins to plate food.

"Parmesan?" He asks and holds up a hand crank cheese grater just like they have in the restaurants. *Who even has stuff like that?*

"Just a little, please."

"Garlic bread?" He asks pointing to a plate of the most delicious bread I've ever seen, adding a slice to his plate.

I look from the bread to his mouth and shake my head no. I watch as he licks his lips and then smiles.

"Yeah, me either," he says pulling the slice off his plate and putting it back with the other pieces.

I'm pretty sure we just confirmed that we'll be making out later, and I almost want to ask if he'd like to skip the meal, but my stomach takes this time to remind me that I skipped lunch as it grumbles loudly. My eyes widen, and I clutch my hands to my stomach.

"I'm glad you're hungry; I've made enough to feed an entire platoon." He hands me a plate before grabbing his own and nodding toward a doorway.

I step into the dining room and look in awe at the beautifully made table. A bottle of wine chills on ice and an amazing array of flowers adorn the center. I wait for him to set his plate down before doing the same at the remaining place setting. Salads are already on the table, and the dressing is in a glass container, and I'm certain I've never had dressing out of anything but the plastic bottle from the store.

I begin to sit down and expectantly, BT is behind me helping me to push my chair to the table. I raise an eyebrow at him as he sits down.

"What?" He asks with a smile wide enough to draw both dimples in his cheeks.

"This may be the most romantic Netflix and Chill I've ever been to."

His smile falls slightly, but he catches himself and reaches to pull the bottle of wine from the ice bucket. "You do this a lot?" I can tell he's trying to act nonchalant about it, but I can hear the concern in his voice.

This is the reason I turned him down as many times as I did. He's a commitment type of guy, and I'm as anti-commitment as they come.

"No, BT," I answer him honestly. "I don't." It's the truth. I've never gone to a man's house under the pretense of "just watching" a movie. The guys who usually come up to me lay their expectations right at my feet. I knew he was different when his initial approach didn't include the words, "hey, wanna fuck?"

I wonder what I've gotten myself into as I watch him pour the wine into both of our glasses, and I want to kick myself for not wanting to get up and leave.

Chapter 3
BT

She was late getting here, and I'd just about convinced myself that her reluctance to say *yes* to coming over had turned into standing me up. Like a teenage boy, my heart was racing when I heard the doorbell, and it continued to race when she reached down and picked Scout up like it was the most natural thing to do.

I had to restrain myself from acting natural when she walked past me, and I got a whiff of her. She is absolutely decadent, but not in an overpowering way. It's almost as if she's covered in oranges and honey, making my mouth water at the urge to lick her and see if she tastes the same.

We make small talk through dinner, and she seems to shut me down each time I ask a question where the answer is more than skin deep. She may not want to talk about her family and such, but her face lights up when I ask about her future. She seems to have things in order as far as which direction she wants her life to go.

"You want to do what?" I ask with eyes widened in shock.

"I want to be a showgirl in Atlantic City," she deadpans.

When I asked what her ultimate goal was after finishing classes, this was not the answer I would've ever guessed.

I run a rough hand over my beard in an attempt to hide my surprise. How she will ever go from the incredibly shy person I met weeks ago to someone who dances all but naked on a huge stage I'll never know.

I see her lip twitch, and I narrow my eyes at her. "You're fucking with me." I smile wide when she grins and begins to laugh.

She wipes her mouth with her napkins and looks back at me. "Could you even picture me dancing on a stage?"

I clear my throat because honestly if I close my eyes I could imagine her doing just about anything. It may not fit her personality, but I have an incredible imagination that could easily formulate a scenario where she's dancing on a stage. I mean it would be a private show just for me, but yeah, I can picture it.

"You had me," I say standing and grabbing our plates. I walk them back to the sink before heading back to the dining room.

"Movie?" I ask as she stands from the table.

"Sure," she says, and I catch a more sultry tone to her voice. I ignore it because if I let myself for a split second think that sex is where tonight is heading, I'll fixate on it and won't be able to carry on a conversation.

"Follow me," I say and head down the hallway.

"Where are we going?" She asks as we bypass the living room and head deeper into the house.

I stop walking and turn back to her. "I don't have a TV in the living room." I shrug. "I don't get the opportunity to watch much because I'm never home, so the only TV I have is in the bedroom."

"Is that right?" I grin at her and nod.

I nod, "I only get to watch a little right before bedtime. Most days there's not even time for that."

She doesn't respond but eventually moves her feet and begins to follow me to the bedroom.

I busy myself with grabbing the remotes from the bedside table and watch her from the corner of my eye as she takes in my inner sanctuary. It's neat but lived in. I make my bed every morning, but it's no longer done with the military precision I was accustomed to while in the service.

I settle on the bed against the headboard and point the remote at the screen. My eyes never leave her as she walks around the end of the bed and climbs on the other side. Even though I know it's awkward to climb in someone else's bed, especially having never even been here before, she takes it in stride and settles again the headboard as well.

I want to shift my body so we're closer together, but I don't. I let her decide if she wants to keep the distance between us. The sight of her legs wrapped in skin tight leggings nearly make me groan. I direct my eyes back to the TV before I make a fool of myself.

"So. *The Office?*" I ask while Netflix loads on the TV.

I catch her watching my face and have to nudge her with my hand to get her attention. "I'm sorry. What?" She asks a little flustered.

I smile big, putting my dimples on full display, well aware of what I'm doing. "Is *The Office* okay?" I ask again.

She shakes her head no, and her gaze leaves mine and refocuses on my lips. My cock jumps in my pants at the thought of her mouth on mine. "I don't want to watch *The Office*," she finally mumbles.

I clear my throat to hide the inevitable huskiness in my voice. It doesn't help one bit. "What do you want to watch?" I ask her mouth because I can't manage to pull my eyes away from it.

"Homework," she pants softly.

That answer makes absolutely no sense. "I don't think that's on Netflix," I answer, distracted.

She briefly cuts her eyes back up to mine and shifts her weight so she's lying back against the pillow. "Let's work on homework."

I stare at her as she makes herself comfortable. All kinds of salacious thoughts are running rampant in my head right now. This beautiful woman is practically lying in my bed; there's no way to keep those kinds of thoughts from happening.

"Homework for tomorrow's class," she says her voice turning as husky as mine is.

I shake my head in an attempt to clear the fog and lust that seems to be swirling around in it. We're working on proper on-screen kissing techniques tomorrow. My eyes widen at her suggestion once my brain finally catches up with her words.

"You want to make out?" I ask stupidly just for clarification.

She bites her lips and dips her head in a quick nod.

"I think that's a great idea," I admit and turn my body so it's facing her more.

I lift my hand up and sweep a strand of hair from the side of her face, but leave my hand in contact with her perfect skin. I groan when she tilts her head slightly, leaning into my touch.

I lean my head closer and whisper, "Want to just go with it or was there a technique you wanted to work on first?"

She licks her lips, and I almost lose all control.

"Camera technique or closed mouth kiss first?" I ask again when she doesn't immediately respond.

I lick my lips in preparation for immediate action once she decides.

"I think the open-mouth kiss is going to be the one we should practice tonight." This woman is my dream come true, and I'm certain each and every one of her rejections up until today was just a way to build the suspense for this exact moment in time.

I groan when she runs her pink tongue over her bottom lip, and my restraint snaps. I place my hands on either side of her legs and bring my mouth to hers. I'm met with the softness of her delicate lips and her quick, soughing breaths.

Call me a wimp if you want to, but I found heaven during Netflix and Chill.

Chapter 4
Aviana

Where the bravery came to ask BT if he wanted to make out came from, I'll never know. He's all for it, of course, and I didn't expect a different response. I also didn't expect his mouth to mold perfectly to mine or how much I enjoyed the soft scratch of his beard against my sensitive skin. I've never kissed a man with a beard before, and after tonight, I don't know that I'd ever want to go back again.

I slant my head slightly to allow him to deepen the kiss. His tongue stroked over mine slowly, but when I placed my hands on his chest, the tremble of his muscles betrayed his barely leashed restraint. Frustratingly, he kept both of his hands flat on the bed by my hips, maintaining his balance when l wanted nothing more than his body weight against mine.

I groan when my slight tug on his shirt doesn't budge him an inch. His smile against my mouth tells me he's well aware of what I want and amused at the frustration I feel with his refusal. I'm seconds away from verbalizing my complaints when I feel the soft stroke of his thumbs against the thin cotton of my leggings.

He pulls his head back a fraction to look at me. I see lust and some other unnamed emotion swim through his eyes as he tries to read my reaction as well.

"You're a very good actor," I admit. My lips are still tingling from the kiss, and my skin hums from the manly roughness where his beard scratched it.

He raises an eyebrow at me. "I wasn't acting." He leans back further looking slightly confused. "Were you?"

I shake my head no, responding honestly. His quick grin shutters his doubt and brings him back into the moment.

I reach my hand up and run my fingers over the scruff that I'm quickly growing a fondness to. "I like this," I admit quietly.

"Then I'll never shave again," he says simply.

My movement stutters briefly. I've grown accustomed to listening and paying attention to each and every thing a man says to me, wary of any promises or misconstrued declarations of future plans. What he just said is almost enough to make me get out of this bed and refuse to speak with him again. He may not mean anything by it, but his simple words displayed more meaning than his conscious self realizes.

BT pulls me from my waring thoughts when his lips gently press against mine. Even his gentle kiss is cause for concern. Most people, when they get together for nothing more than a fun time, go at each other like maniacs, as if they'll never get another chance; which is exactly what my intentions are.

Knowing this, I deepen the kiss and give it an edge of violence and aggression. I fist the front of his shirt and pull him forcefully against me. He leans in further than before but still refuses the full contact I'm seeking. His kiss turns feverish, and I take it as a good sign. I want him wild and lustful; it's the soft and sweet that I can't handle. Those types of kisses lead to emotions I have no desire of investigating, no matter how much I like his beard.

"Touch me," I beg against his lips before delving back in again tangling my tongue with his.

He groans into my mouth and brings one hand up to cup my cheek. This man is absolutely frustrating. I'm in his bed after weeks of him relentlessly pursuing me, and he's practically refusing to give me exactly what I know we both want.

I literally take matters into my own hands by reaching up and palming his cock through his jeans. He's hard and thick and obviously ready for what I have in mind. He moans, and I feel his hips shift, pressing himself tighter against my hand. My lower body tingles and my clit throbs, demanding attention. *Now this is more like it.*

I release my grip on his shirt and use both hands to work the button and zipper open on his jeans. He pulls away from my mouth and looks down at me. His panting breaths are forceful enough to sway the hair at my temples. Releasing my face, he covers my hands with his.

"Slow down," he says gently.

What? Slow down? Who the hell slows down at a moment like this?

I tilt my head, realizing I'm now the one that's confused. "You don't want to...?" I angle my head down and wiggle my fingers under his.

He huffs as if I've just said the most insane thing ever, and I grin, certain he's going to let me continue.

He bursts my bubble when he asks, "What's the rush?"

How do I tell him this is his only chance? How do I explain to him that I don't do relationships and a second "date" with him will never happen, especially since it's obvious he's a relationship kind of guy?

"I want you," I tell him and nip at his jaw playfully.

"And I want you, but that's not what tonight is about, Aviana."

"But it could be." I'm practically begging him, and I don't beg. I'm not the type of girl who's ever needed to explain why sex is the best course of action to a guy. I've never had to, and I wouldn't be now if I hadn't had the opportunity to grip what he has concealed behind the denim of his blue jeans. My mouth waters at the idea of doing more with it than gripping it through his jeans.

"Not tonight," he says, and I can hear a small tinge of regret in his voice.

I nod my head in understanding and turn my eyes from his to focus on the menu screen of Netflix on the TV across the room.

"I should go." I pull my hands back from the erection that's all for what I have in mind and place them on my lap.

"We can still make out," he says hope apparent in his tone.

I slide off the bed. "I have an early class tomorrow," I explain.

It's only nine o'clock, but he doesn't call me out on it. His face falls marginally, disappointment evident in his eyes.

"I'll walk you to the door." He stands on the other side of the bed and gestures with his hand for me to go first. From the corner of my eye as I pass him in the hallway, I see him adjust himself in his jeans. For a split second I hope he changes his mind, but I know me leaving is the best thing. I don't use guys any more than they use me, and I know if I stay and push the issue, the tables would no longer be balanced.

Can I convince him to sleep with me tonight? Of course I can; he's a man. I don't mean that in a bad way, but my experience tells me that men have less control over their restraint than they want to believe. I'm certain if I strip out of my clothes, walk to him naked, and reach for his zipper, he'd give me free range. But then tomorrow, he would be in a different place than I will be. He'll expect things to continue even if it were casual, and I would be done.

Once we reach the door, he grabs my purse from the entryway closet and opens the door.

"Hey," he says getting my attention before I can flee down the front walkway.

I turn to him, and he gently kisses my lips. "See you tomorrow in class," he whispers against my lips.

I give him a weak smile, and turn and walk toward my car.

Tomorrow is going to be one awkward situation. I knew I should've listened to my gut and refused to come over. I knew he'd take the hint and give up eventually. The sincerity and promise in his eyes earlier in class got me. I have to remind myself repeatedly on the drive back to my crappy apartment that it's always the charming devils that bring the most pain.

I'm in my own little world as I pull up outside my dimly lit apartment. BT asked me what I wanted to do with my life in regards to the acting classes I've been taking. I told a joke about being a showgirl to throw him off of the conversation, and thankfully it worked.

Admitting that acting classes are the only form of school I could afford, and even though I have no desire to be an actress, some education is better than none. I really wanted to go into sports medicine, but being the girl from the wrong side of the tracks from a broken family didn't actually pay for medical school now did it?

Throwing myself a pity party as I make my way to the stairs to my second-floor apartment wasn't the smartest. I always pay attention to what I'm doing and my surroundings. BT and the events of tonight are bouncing around my head. I shouldn't allow myself to be so distracted. Especially not when arms reach out and grab me from behind. Seconds is all it took for my mouth to be taped and a rough canvas bag to be thrown over my head. Fighting was futile against the strength of the man who held me captive, but I gave it my all.

I should've stayed and made out with BT is the last thought that runs through my head just before darkness takes over.

Chapter 5
BT

I hardly got a wink of sleep last night after Aviana left. I've never had a situation go completely off the rails as fast as it did last night. I was trying to be a gentleman. I thought if she knew I didn't invite her over just for sex she'd be more willing to see me again. What I didn't expect was for her to get up and leave because I told her as much.

I texted her last night asking her to let me know she made it home and expressed how enjoyable I thought the evening had been. She didn't respond back and for the life of me, I couldn't figure out where I went wrong.

Hoping today doesn't turn completely awkward, I make my way to class with several ideas of how to broach the subject once we're broken off in pairs. I'm running late, which is not the norm for me, but there was horrible traffic on the way to the acting studio, and I didn't allow for the time.

I had less than three minutes to spare before the start of class. My temperament had seen better days when I walked into class, and a quick sweep of the room informed me that Aviana wasn't even in class today. I took my normal seat when all I felt like doing was skipping and heading to the gym.

Was last night so bad that she's skipping today to avoid me?

I scrub my hands over my beard in frustration but have to smile remembering her say how much she liked it.

The instructor breezes into the classroom and gives direction on what we'll be doing for the next week. Kissing. It's in the syllabus. We knew it was coming. From the moans and mild clapping around the room, I could tell it is possibly the most liked as well as most hated topic to work on.

My eyes dart around the room once more hoping that Aviana would appear. I know if I ever get an acting job I'll have to do this sort of thing with other women, but I have no desire to touch my lips to anyone else's but hers.

"Want to partner up?" I hear from beside me.

I look to my right and see a cute brunette with a severe blunt cut bob and so much shine in her eyes it's hard to look away. She's hopeful I'll say yes as she twists her hands together, wringing her fingers against each other. She looks almost devious right now, and even though I know it's a horrible idea, I'm not a complete asshole. *It's only class, right?*

"Sure," I tell her trying not to sound completely put out.

She squirms in her seat like she's won the damn lottery as I turn my attention back to the teacher who's informing us that we will be working on camera technique kissing. This is the best news I've heard all day. At least with this type of kissing, we don't have to touch each other's mouths. Camera technique is all about making it look like a couple is kissing. The angle of the camera shows the back of the head and has more to do with the placement of the shot rather than the actual physical act of kissing.

As usual, several tripods are set up around the room, and we go to the corner where Aviana and I always go. The cameras are digital, but we turn them on to record, so later we can see ourselves and work on perfecting whichever acting technique we are learning.

I turn the camera on as I walk by and wait for the next instruction from the teacher.

"I want the males back to the cameras first," the teacher says. I work on getting in place and notice just how tall my partner is. I won't have to bend down hardly at all to make this look right. It's a plus for today I guess, and I try to hide my disappointment in not working with Aviana.

"Sheryl, you can have your back facing the shot first since you're partnered up with Samantha today," I hear the teacher say directing another set of students. I look over and cock an eyebrow at the pair of girls as they get ready to get to work. I could watch those girls make out all damn day.

I hear a throat beside me clear, pulling my attention away from the two blonde bombshells who are about to practice a kissing scene. I chuckle lightly as I see several of the other guys in class more concerned over the lesbian kiss that's about to take place than the girls that are standing in front of them.

What can I say? We're men.

"Positions!" I hear the teacher say with a less than enthusiastic tone.

I turn back to my partner and roll my shoulders, preparing to get this class over with.

"I'm Candy by the way," my kissing partner for the day says with an outstretched hand.

I shake her hand. "BT," I tell her. "You ready?"

She shakes her head enthusiastically. She steps in closer to me and reaches her hands up to twine in my hair. Licking her lips, she says, "I'm more than ready."

Where the fuck is Aviana?

"Action!" The teacher says.

I lean my body closer into Candy and place my hands on her neck mimicking her stance. I stop a few inches from her mouth as the instructions in the book said is required for a camera technique kiss. This girl goes all out and crashes her lips against mine, and before I can protest, she's got her tongue in my damn mouth!

My eyes widen, and I push her away gently. "What the hell?" I say more than a little annoyed.

She shrugs her shoulders. "We're at kissing practice," she says.

"That's not the technique we're supposed to be practicing right now," I huff with more force in my voice than I probably should have after being kissed so feverishly by a woman most men would consider a perfect ten. I wipe at my mouth with the back of my hand, and she has the gall to look offended.

I'm not an idiot. I know that the women at the acting studio talk about me all the time. I ignore the gossip and their attention. Strangely enough, the more I ignore it, the more they seem to gossip. It's gotten so bad that some of the guys sneer at me when I walk past as if I can control them and the shit they say about me. Last week I was most decidedly gay, and today Candy has taken it upon herself to shove her tongue down my fucking throat.

"Can we just work on this?" I ask as she stares at me with her arms crossed over her chest like I'd just attacked her mouth without invitation.

She gets a sly smile on her face which forces me to hold a finger up stopping her as she slinks closer to me. "Camera technique," I remind her.

This is possibly the most torture I've suffered in acting class and for the briefest of seconds, I wish I was back in the sands of the Middle East.

***

I text Aviana again after leaving class. I do it jokingly, but I let her know that she was truly missed, and I had to suffer through Candy's attack since she wasn't there. She doesn't respond. I get a sinking feeling in my gut as over the next couple of days she doesn't show up at class or respond to my text messages.

I do my best to keep busy at the gym. We've had a few guys come in with a real desire to get fit before they head off to basic. I love working with these guys the most. I'm a patriot through and through, and I know that level of pride for my country sticks with them, even when I can tell at first they almost want to back out when they discover the injury I suffered while at war.

It's been nearly ten years since Hell rained down on me in the desert, and although a loss of a limb has become my new normal, I know I'd still be in the middle of the war with sand in my ass if my Humvee wasn't targeted and struck with an IED.

Even with the new guys I'm training to get in top physical shape, I can't seem to shake the eeriness over Aviana's absence from class. She's been gone from class now for three days, and I know that even our evening, which I'm now considering a disaster, is not bad enough to keep her from more than a half a week of class.

I realize, as I try to make a plan to reach out to her, that I don't know anything about her other than her phone number and the way her mouth fits perfectly against mine. I plan to ask around tomorrow at class. I know a few girls I've seen her talking to in class, and I hope to hell they know something about her. If they don't, I may have to consider even more drastic measures, like breaking into the registrar's office to get her home address.

It would be pretty shameful for a Purple Heart Recipient to get arrested for burglary, but it's a chance I'm willing to take if only to make sure she's okay and not in some sort of harm.

Chapter 6
Aviana

The sound of hushed voices registers in my ears as I try to force some form of cognizant thought into my brain. The neighbors usually aren't this damn noisy, but as more of the elderly in the building either die or get moved to assisted living, the tenants get younger and apparently louder. I've lived in this building for two years, and if I could afford to live in a nicer place, I'd jump at the opportunity. I know, however, that's not going to happen anytime soon.

I roll over and resist the urge to pound on the wall and tell them all to shut the fuck up. At the end of the day, they're my neighbors, and the last thing someone should do is piss off the people who live right next door, especially when you share a wall with them.

I try to force my eyes open and realize how heavy they feel. I reach back into my subconscious and try to figure out if I drank a lot last night. My tongue seems thicker than usual, I have a pounding headache, and stiffness in my bones even the most expensive massage could never work out.

I crack my eyes and do my best to sit up on my bed. They widen painfully as I realize I'm not home. The room is dark, but I can tell immediately that the room I'm in is most definitely not mine. My pulse pounds in my ears as I try to remember what happened last night.

I look beside me and feel a wave of relief wash over me as I find myself alone in bed. Only once before had I woken up with only vague memories of my night with some guy I had no idea his name or how I came to be naked beside me. The incident lead to months of blood work and finally relief over not contracting some fucked up STD. I vowed then and there that I'd never put myself in a situation like that again, which is why I'm so freaked out right now.

"Think, Avi," I mutter to myself.

I hiss when a vague memory of leaving BT's house hits me. I know I made it home then…

I cup my hands over my mouth as a guttural scream escapes my lips. I was attacked last night. Through tears and shame, I inventory my body. Other than my headache and the disgusting taste in my mouth, I'm still wearing my clothes from last night. This gives me hope that nothing, well other than being abducted, happened against my will.

I bring my knees to my chest and hug my arms around them just as a door opens, and a looming shadow stands in the doorway. I raise an arm to shield my eyes against the blinding light.

"She's awake, Boss," the man in the doorway says over his shoulder.

I shrink back and make myself as small as possible as he steps out of the way and another man walks further into the room. He reaches a hand out and flips the light switch, casting the room in the harshest light I've ever encountered.

I tuck my mouth and nose into my knees but keep my eyes on him, terrified what will happen if I look away. I have no idea how to react to a situation like this, but I know turning your attention away from it will only keep me from seeing what will happen.

"Hello, Aviana Maguire." His voice is two packs a day rough, and I cringe at the thought of him coming closer to me.

I'm not an idiot; I know what happens to girls who get abducted. I vow to myself that I'll die before I let one of them touch me or hurt me like that.

"I'm Vito," he continues.

"Why am I here?" My voice is shaking which makes me feel weak, but I can't help the tremble in it while this huge guy, in a suit of all things, stands in front of me.

"Mitch Maguire is your dad, right?" I narrow my eyes.

"Clearly I wouldn't be here if you weren't sure," I spit at him. I'd like to say that I have no idea where the sudden fierceness came from, but knowing this has to do with my dad, makes me seethe with anger.

"Firecracker," he says with mild approval. "I like that." He smiles at me, and I curl even further into myself. "Your dad owes the SINdicate a lot of money, sweet girl."

His pet name makes my skin crawl. I don't want him to think I'm sweet. I want him to see me as vile as I see him.

"Still doesn't explain why *I'm* here," I say even though it's clear he's gotten his ass in some hot water.

He tilts his head to the side as if I know what's going on with my father.

"Look," I say trying to sound like a voice of reason. "I haven't seen my dad in fourteen years, and I've only spoken to him on the phone like three times after he disappeared when I was eleven. The only reason why I've spoken to him at all is because he sought me out hoping I'd loan him some money."

His face remains impassive as I throw out the information from my fucked up, nonexistent relationship with my father.

"If you let me go, I won't tell anyone what happened," I reason with him. "This is clearly a misunderstanding. I don't have any money, so I can't pay you whatever it is that he owes."

He grunts and rubs his face with his hand. The gleam of the light reflects off of an expensive watch. How much could he possibly owe that would cause thugs to abduct a woman? This man clearly has money. His suit is designer, and if the watch is any indication, I'm certain his cufflinks are platinum as well.

"That's not how it works, sweet girl. Your dad owes my boss over two hundred thousand. That's not an amount we can just let slide." He clasps his hands in front of him and waits for my reaction.

Tears roll down my face. "I don't have that kind of money," I admit knowing that there is no telling what will happen to me once the words leave my lips.

"We know that. We've been following you for days."

I gasp. Days? How did I not know I was being watched? Don't people get like a sixth sense and feel creeped out when someone is following them?

"If you know I don't have the money, then why am I here?"

My attention is pulled from him to the open doorway where I see two women pass in some of the skimpiest clothes I've ever laid my eyes on, and that's saying something. I live in Tampa after all.

I cut my eyes back to him when a horrible thought comes to me. "I'll die before you turn me into a fucking hooker," I say with renewed hatred.

His laugh catches me off guard, and even more so when his head tilts back, and he clutches at his chest as if I'd just told the most hilarious joke. He calms quicker than I'd thought possible after such a boisterous explosion of laughter.

"Well, sweet girl," he says wiping his eyes as if his amusement brought tears to them. "If you do as you're told, and your dad gets the money together quickly, we won't have to resort to turning you out."

My hands tremble as I clutch my forearms around my knees. "Where am I? Last time I talked to my dad, he wasn't in Florida."

"You're not in Florida anymore either," he says as he turns and walks away.

He shuts the door softly behind him. If he wasn't endangering my life or threatening to make me a hooker, I could easily admit how handsome he was, but the look in his eyes and his apparent ease at criminal activity makes him the most dangerous man I've ever met.

He gave no directions. He didn't explain what is expected of me. He just left. I realize then that I'm doomed. There is no way in hell my dad will have the ability to come up with two hundred thousand dollars. Even if he could, he'd never use it to rescue a daughter he's had no involvement with the last decade and a half.

I cry harder when the reminder that I have no true friends hits me. There's no one to miss me. No one that will even bat an eyelash when I don't show up for work. The turnover at the hotel is so high; they have people waiting on standby when employees don't show up for their shift.

BT invades my thoughts. I wish I'd stayed longer at his house. I'm not a fool. I know with the information that they've been watching me for days meant this situation would've happened eventually. Short of my dad paying the money before they took me, this would have happened regardless, but having a few more memories of BT would've been nice before facing the hell I'm sure to encounter.

I can't quit. I can't give up. I know I have to fight even though I have no idea where I am or what kind of resources this SINdicate that Vito mentioned has. I have to either get out of here or die trying. I don't imagine Vito is going to remain as cordial as he was this evening. It's only a matter of time before they realize my father won't pay the money, and that's when my time runs out.

Chapter 7
BT

Four days of Aviana not showing up for class is my limit. It's not that she may have just dropped out, she hasn't responded to a single one of my texts, which have grown increasingly desperate over the last thirty-six hours.

I ask around the class, and the people I speak with have no real information about her. She's kept to herself so much it seems she has no friends, well at the acting academy anyways. I haven't met a girl yet who doesn't have at least one friend they're super close to. It seems that friend of hers doesn't take classes here.

After another long day of kissing techniques classes, I'm ready to bust into the registrar's office like I'd contemplated a few days ago. Thank God I didn't get stuck with Candy. I've been partnered up with another girl who seems to sincerely want to learn in class, so I haven't gotten attacked like I did that very first day.

I gather my things at the end of class and begin to walk out of the room. A petite blonde is waiting outside the door, and not the petite blonde I've been thinking of relentlessly for the past several days. We have another class together, but she's not in the one I just finished. She's not one of the ones I usually see talking in a group or snickering with the other girls, so her being here, apparently waiting for me, is quite out of character.

"Hey," she says as she pushes herself off of the wall.

I greet her but keep walking, and she falls into step with me.

"Heard you were asking around about Aviana."

I stop in my tracks and turn her direction, giving her one hundred percent of my attention.

"She's not been in class for a few days. I'm worried about her."

She shifts her books from her side to the front of her chest. The act is clearly a safety mechanism.

"She lives in my building," she says. "I don't know which apartment is hers, but I haven't seen her in a few days either. We sometimes walk back from class, but she lives on a higher floor, so I have no clue which apartment is actually hers."

I want to reach out and hug this girl! This is the best news I've had in days.

"You walk? So the apartment is close?"

She points down the street. "Goldenbriar Apartments. Just right down the road a few blocks."

I don't even bother with grabbing my truck. I thank the girl and take off toward the apartment complex, trying to figure out a way to get her apartment number. I'm not familiar with the complex, but I know even shitty apartment managers just don't hand out apartment numbers. Maybe fifty bucks would work? I'll give everything in my wallet to get the information I need.

I head to the front of the complex looking for the office, hoping the manager inside is a woman. I'll use every ounce of charm that I have to get the information I need. *I hope they're a fan of beards.*

I stop short when I reach the front door to the office. The notification on the door is weathered and seems to be old, having suffered the elements longer than the information leads you to believe. The office is closed today because the manager is sick. The sign has clearly been hanging for weeks if not longer. Thankfully, a phone number has been given to reach the complex manager.

I pull out my phone and call the number. The office being closed is a blessing in disguise.

The first call goes to voicemail, so I hang up and immediately call again. After five rings the second time around a man answers the phone. He doesn't sound sick, but he does sound drunk.

"What?" he asks.

"Hey man, thank God!" I act much more enthused than I'm feeling, hating that Aviana is stuck living in such a shit hole.

"What do you want?"

"I have a flower delivery for Aviana Maguire, and the asshole who ordered them didn't leave an apartment number. Think you can help me out?"

"Maguire? Is that the hot little blonde that's only about five feet tall?"

I want to say yes, but honestly, a delivery guy wouldn't have a clue what she looks like. I swallow my rage at knowing this nasty fucker has been watching her. "Yeah, probably," I finally respond.

He stays silent, and I can't tell if he's going to refuse or if he honestly just doesn't know.

"Listen, man. You'd be doing me a real solid. My boss is already on my ass about me taking a few extra breaks last week. I can't lose this job. My old lady will have my ass if I get fired again." *If you can't beat the filth, join them I guess.*

"Yeah," he agrees. "I totally get the boss and the bitch riding a man's back. She's in 4F."

I hang up without saying thank you, and I don't even feel sorry about it.

I walk around the complex and see Aviana's car parked in the parking lot. With hopeful steps, I make my way to the inner courtyard where the stairs are. A huge concrete square in the center leads me to believe that there was a pool there at one point, but it has been filled in and covered over. I'd actually be amazed if a shitty place like this had a pool, so seeing this comes as no surprise. Pools, even in Tampa, are expensive as hell to maintain, and by the looks of this place, maintenance is the last thing going on.

I feel like I'm risking my life as I climb the iron and concrete stairs to the fourth floor. There are bolts missing and welds coming apart every few steps, and I have no idea how this place ever could've passed a safety inspection. She lives on the top floor. If there was ever a fire in this place, she'd be a sitting duck. I know a lot of college students live in shitty places; Tampa is an expensive place to live, but knowing Aviana is forced to come home to a shit hole like this every day has me wanting to insist she move in with me, if anything as a roommate just to get her out of this place.

The thought strikes a chord with me. I've always been an advocate of women. It's the least I can do. I can find beauty in every woman I've ever encountered if their personalities don't interfere too much. Some women ruin it with the way they act. Aviana is more than beauty to me. She's gorgeous don't get me wrong, but I feel very protective of her. This isn't brotherly intention. This isn't a simple man being protective of a woman. *Fuck, her kiss ruined me.*

A creepy, uneasy feeling washes over me as I approach her door. Her apartment isn't actually labeled, but it is situated between the apartments labeled 4E and 4G. The door is slightly askew which has my hackles up.

Aviana may not be able to help where she lives, but even the small amount of time I spent with her lets me know she's not dumb. She'd never be home, in this neighborhood, with her door not only unlocked but slightly open.

My hand immediately finds the Sig 1911s at my hip. Expecting to find her apartment ransacked, I slowly push the door open with my foot. The apartment has been rummaged through, and it is absolutely filthy. The smell coming from the inside reminds me of hot garbage before the trash trucks make their way through town in the summer.

I do my best to keep my free hand away from my mouth and nose. I'm not a stranger to stinky shit. Years in the Army and tours in the Middle East introduced me to some of the most disgusting sights and smells one could even imagine, but it's been almost ten years since I was flown out of there. Somehow my senses have readjusted to disallow the disgusting smells.

    I inch slowly through the apartment and stop short when I see some homeless man laid out on the couch. I instantly wonder if he's dead and if that's what is causing the rancid stench in the house, but I see his chest rising a fraction. I cut my eyes to the table and see the burned out spoon and hypodermic needle that's clearly been used a dozen too many times. The only thing missing is the tourniquet for this junkie. Looking back at the man on the couch, I see the thin rubber tubing tied loosely around his arm.

    I leave him because without interruption, he's not going anywhere anytime soon. I creep through the apartment, clearing the bathroom, and what I presume is her bedroom if the turquoise sheets and comforter are any indication. Clearly this man has been squatting here, and the condition of her apartment is not of her doing. Someone who buys matching sheets and curtains wouldn't live in these conditions.

    I check the bathtub, closets, and I even crouched down and looked under the bed, relieved at not finding a body. Consequently, there isn't any blood that I can see either. The entire apartment has been completely pillaged and there's no chance of really finding any real evidence that would lead anywhere in this mess.

    I head back out into the living room and kick the guy with my boot.

    "Wake the fuck up!" I say still training my weapon on him. "Now!" I yell and kick him again.

    He stirs, but I have to shove him with my foot repeatedly before he finally sits up on the couch.

    "What are you doing here?" I watch as he scrubs his dirty beard with his hands. Just watching him makes my own face itch.

    "I live here," he mumbles.

    "Like fuck you do!" I don't know what concerns me most, him lying to me or his lack of concern that I have a weapon pointed at his head.

    He doesn't respond again, and I know I didn't ask a question, but this asshole better get to speaking. I'm twitchy and even with my training, twitchy is never good.

    "Where's the girl?" His eyes dart up to mine and for the first time, there's an honest reaction out of him. I narrow my own eyes and try to determine if its guilt over doing something wrong or relief that someone else is here to help.

"They took her," he sobs. "They stole my baby girl, and it's all my fault!"

Chapter 8
Aviana

As hard as it is to keep track of time while inside a building every second of every day, I know I have been here for four or five days. I haven't seen Vito since his first visit, which is a blessing and a curse. I don't know why I'm holding out hope that my father will somehow manage to get his hands on the money that is owed.

At this point, I'm hoping his dumb ass successfully robs a bank, but I know having that much money in his hands would be a temptation he wouldn't be able to fight, even when his daughter's life is on the line.

What the hell did I ever do to deserve such shitty parents? Who decides who gets who? I want to talk to their manager because I think a refund is in order.

Even though I'm not confined to my room, I've stayed in here as much as possible. I didn't leave for the longest time until the growling in my stomach was louder than the raging thoughts in my head.

It was apparent very quickly that the rooms have been roughly converted from a wing of a hotel. There is a thick steel door that I've never seen opened that appears to be the only exit out of here. There is a living room type of space situated around that door that seems to have been created by the walls of several of the hotel rooms being knocked out. One straight, long hallway leads to other rooms. These are inhabited by the other women who stay here. They have their private areas just as I have mine.

Walking out of my room that first time wasn't as traumatizing as I had anticipated it being. The other women milling around, although not overly friendly, didn't seem to be bitter for being here. I stopped and asked one girl close to my age when we would get to eat. She pointed down the hall without another word.

I slowly covered the length of the hallway with small steps, praying a door doesn't swing open. I'm terrified someone is going to grab me and do the things to me that my mind has created. Close to the end of the hall, I found a large room without a door. I wish I could tell you that the entryway was nice and transitioned gracefully from the hall into the room but it wasn't. The door had literally been pulled off of the hinges indicating, I suppose, that this was considered a public area for all the women to utilize.

Cautiously, I look around the room looking for a sign or rules to follow about how to utilize the kitchen or if things are off limits. I'm hungry, but I don't want to piss anyone off or earn some sort of punishment for actions I should know are banned. I find nothing posted and that actually fills me with more trepidation than ease. I hate the unknown.

    My stomach growls, forcing me into action and not giving a shit if there will be consequences. I pull open the cabinets and find them stuffed with food. The pantry to the left of the refrigerator reveals the same thing. Granted, the majority of the food is organic and considered healthy, not exactly what you want to eat when you're throwing yourself a pity party. I'm not bitching about food being available, but I was hoping more for Doritos or chocolate, not rice cakes and protein bars.

    Digging around a little more, I decide on a Nutella and jelly sandwich and a ranch flavored rice cake. I know I was bitching before, but it is damn near a gourmet meal when the flavor hits my tongue. I'm sitting at one of the tables adjacent to the kitchen area. Once again, I don't know if eating in the rooms are allowed, but I don't want to get into trouble. The tables are clearly here to be eaten on, so I figure they're safe.

    I'm scarfing down my food, not only because I feel like I'm starving but also because I want to get out of here before anyone else comes in. My face falls when another girl walks in and grabs a disgustingly green *Naked* juice from the fridge. I cringe when she saunters across the room and takes a seat across from me. Of all the other spots to pick, she sits right near me.

    I'm torn in this situation. I want to find out information and do my best to figure out a way to get out of this place, but I also have no clue who I can trust. She looks nice enough, but that doesn't mean a damn thing. She also doesn't look like she's being forced to be here, and that can't be a good sign.

    She's taller than I am and quite a bit curvier. Her large breasts are hugged generously by her thin tank top. She's not wearing a bra and by the looks of things she either has the best set of natural boobs I've ever seen or she has implants.

    "I'm Darby," she says softly after giving me enough time to take her in.

    "Aviana," I tell her and immediately wonder if I should've given her a fake name. No sense in that I guess since Vito knows exactly who I am.

    "How long is your contract?" I give her a blank stare. *What in the world is she talking about?*

"Contract?" I say with a confused shake of my head.

"Yeah, the contract."

"I didn't sign a contract." She snaps her head up from where she was focusing on peeling the label of her juice bottle. Now she's the one confused.

"Really?"

I'm surprised they have no clue that I'm being held here against my will. "That Vito guy," I begin before she interrupts me.

"Mmm," she fake moans softly. "Vito's my favorite. He's a good tipper too."

Good tipper? What. The. Fuck?

I feel like I've somehow woken up in the damn Twilight Zone.

"Vito had me abducted because my dad owes him money. I don't even know where I am," I explain.

I watch as her face falls slightly. "Yeah, we get girls like you every once in a while." She takes a small sip of her drink, and I can tell she's contemplating on whether or not to tell me more. "You're in Las Vegas."

"Vegas?" My dad owes money to people in Vegas? No wonder the amount was so high. You wouldn't find someone dumb enough to give that type of money to him in Tampa.

"What kind of place is this?" I ask hoping she'll keep talking. I still haven't decided if she can be trusted, so the less I say and the more she shares is best.

She gets a look in her eye like she's trying to make it sound better than it actually is, which makes me suddenly even more uncomfortable.

"It's sort of like a brothel." I gasp, and she has the wherewithal to scrunch her nose up because that sounds pretty damn bad.

"A whore house?" I ask completely appalled. Why the hell would Vito bring me to a whore house? There's no way I'm going to whore myself out.

"I mean if you want it to sound really bad, then I guess you could label it a whore house." She uses finger quotes on whore house, and it makes me grin.

"Fuck," I say in a rush. "I mean, I'm not judging you but, really?"

She shrugs her shoulders as if she's used to my response. "Honestly, sucking dick is better than being homeless."

I nod in agreement, but inside I'm wondering if that's true. I live in a shitty apartment, but the roof doesn't leak, and it's warm inside when it's cold out. I have no idea what it would be like when you're homeless so I can't really judge her for her choices.

"You're here by choice then?" She nods. "What happens if you don't want to… you know…?"

"Suck 'em and fuck 'em?" She grins. "Some women don't last long here, and they take them away."

"So they force you to have sex with them?" I push my unfinished plate of food away. Even as hungry as I know I am, I couldn't stomach another bite after the information she's just put at my feet.

"They don't force us, Aviana. Besides," she says as she stands from the table. "The guys treat us well, most of them are incredibly handsome, and a couple of them are even good in bed."

She begins to walk back out of the room, and I hope I haven't offended her by my reaction. I hope she knows that although she's here by choice, I'm not. This isn't something I've chosen for myself.

"Darby?" She turns back to me. "Who are they and why does this place even exist?"

She lowers her head slightly before she speaks. "They're the SINdicate, and most of them work so much they don't have time to date. We're here so they can blow off steam quickly and then get back to work."

She gives me a quick smile and waggles her fingers in a quick wave, and she leaves me in the room alone. Now the racing thoughts from earlier are much worse now that some facts have been added. I needed a plan to get out of here more, now than ever.

Chapter 9
BT

I watch as the broken man in front of me sobs for his daughter. I give him a few minutes to compose himself, but when it becomes clear that he won't be able to without intervention, I clear my throat.

He pops his head up and looks in my direction as if he's just remembered that I'm standing here.

"Who took her?" I ask and follow his hands as he begins to scratch at existing sores on his arm, his nails causing new ones as well.

He shakes his head as if he's going to refuse to give the information. I raise my gun slightly higher. It's a scare tactic that I hope works because I know I'd never be able to shoot the man. Even if he is a disgusting tweaker whom I'm certain is somehow the cause of Aviana's disappearance, I won't shoot her dad. Unless he tries to attack me, then I'd shoot him. Adrenaline rushes quickly in my blood, and the faintest plea in the back of my head begs for a quick second for him to make a move.

I shake my head to clear the thoughts as best I can.

"I suggest you tell me." I pause trying to keep my finger on the trigger guard rather than on the actual trigger.

"I got into some trouble. They took her as payment." He sobs again, but he's so dehydrated, he's run out of tears.

"What the fuck are you talking about, old man? You sold your fucking daughter?" He's even more vile than his outward appearance led me to believe.

"Might as well have sold her!" He yells suddenly getting angry. *Get off the couch; I fucking dare you.* "They want me to pay two hundred thousand dollars. I don't have that kind of money. She's theirs. There's nothing I can do."

Ignoring the details I ask, "Who do you owe that kind of money to?"

His head jerks up like I've thrown something at him. "I can't tell you that." His eyes widen even further, "They'll kill me."

"Look at you. Seems like death would be easier than the shit you're dealing with now." I should regret saying such a horrible thing. It may not have been drugs in my life, but I've been pretty fucking close to rock bottom myself. I know the kinds of thoughts he's thinking. Only difference is, my rock bottom didn't cause harm or even possible death to others.

He nods his head as if agreeing that death would be easier. "Can you find her?"

"I sure as hell will give it my best." It's an honest answer. I can't be sure of much else until I know exactly what it is that I'm dealing with.

I watch as he takes a small bag out of the front pocket of his shirt. "They call themselves the SINdicate." He taps the bag, so some of the hard clumps fall out onto the scorched spoon I'd seen on the table earlier. Because getting high right now is the best thing for his daughter apparently. "They're out of Vegas."

"What casino?" He ignores me as he scoops up the lighter from the table. "Stop!" I insist. "You're not smoking that shit with me in here."

"Then get the fuck out," he seethes. I can already see the tremble in his hand and know he's not far off from losing it. He probably should have taken his next hit an hour ago.

"Tell me what I want to know," I say through gritted teeth.

He ignores me for the last time, and I take a step forward just as he lifts the lighter under the spoon. I kick the shit out of his hands before he has time to strike the flint.

"What the fuck have you done?" I shake my head, growing angrier every second, as I watch him scramble after the small pellets of dope on the disgusting carpet.

"Tell me what I need to know, old man or I'll take what's left from your pocket." He turns suddenly and clutches his dirty hand over the pocket on his shirt. I almost laugh because he looks exactly like Sméagol off of *Lord of the Rings* when he finally got his hand on the little, golden ring. Except this shit isn't funny and Aviana's life is in danger. If she's still alive, comes to my head unbidden.

"What Casino?"

"It's called The Golden Dragon."

"Never heard of it." I've been to Vegas numerous times, and it doesn't ring a bell.

"It's not on the strip. It's mainly used by locals and people..." His voice trails off, but I see his fingers twitch against his chest.

"You smoked two hundred thousand in dope?" I don't even try to hide the disdain in my voice.

"I gambled some too," he says sounding affronted.

"You went there looking for drugs?"

"I went there broke. They found me, not the other way around," he explains. This means they're looking for people to get their hooks into.

I nod, scenarios already running through my head. I need to get out of here and start putting a fucking plan together. I'm already days behind.

"How long did they give you?"

"Three weeks." His fingers dip into his front pocket as if it's second nature and the action is subconscious.

"Mother fucker," I mumble as I holster the Sig.

"You going to go find my baby girl?" The packet of dope is already open and tipped over the top of the spoon.

"You better be gone before I get back. This is the last fucking thing she needs to see after what you've put her through."

I leave him in the squalor of the apartment. I have more important things to deal with, and her useless father is the last fucking thing on my list.

***

I make my way back to campus to get my truck. The dank air from the apartment clings to me, and the urge to head home to take a shower is almost too hard to resist.

My first call is to my boss at the Academy. I tell him there's been a family emergency, and I have to take a leave of absence. He doesn't give me any shit and doesn't ask questions. The next call I place will not go as quickly, so I pull up an old friend's number and put the other call on the back burner.

The phone rings several times before being answered. "What's wrong," the man on the other end of the call says with no other greeting.

"Why does something have to be wrong?" I ask even though I know what he's going to say.

"You never call. Something must be wrong." I instantly wish I'd been a better friend to him. My life is busy, and I'm sure his is too, but I should make more time for the people in my life.

"Spill it, peg leg." I smile from ear to ear. Anyone else saying something like that to me would piss me off at the audacity, but since Blade is a double-leg amputee, he had one leg up on me, or was it down? At any rate, this man knows better than most what's it's like to be in our situation and sometimes, well most of the time, comedy is the best answer.

I'm just about to brag about half priced pedicures, but the realization that Aviana's gone and I'm just wasting time right now hits me hard.

"I need some help," I pause. "I need some things, but more importantly, I need a secure line for Shadow."

"Pretty serious then, huh?" He asks, and I can hear him rustling paper around.

"Extremely serious," I tell him.

He rattles off the number to me, and I jot it down on a receipt in the console of my truck. "Grab a burner before you call him."

"Of course," I say. "We'll catch up after this."

"It'll be good to see that ugly, bearded face of yours," he says with a chuckle.

We hang up, and I head for the nearest store that sells prepaid phones. At each stop light on my way, I begin deleting and suspending each one of my social media pages. Not to brag, but my face has been all over the internet for years. I hope the assholes in Vegas don't recognize me. I'm pretty certain that they don't read romance novels, so that's a plus.

I shoot off quick messages to the authors I have pending shoots for and let the photographers know I have some shit to deal with. I assure them I'll be back before long, and we'll pick up right where I left off. Everyone seems to be super understanding, and that's what I love about the indie author world.

I contemplate calling the police, but I know they can't help me. This became Federal jurisdiction when they took her over state lines. Well, I presume they took her back to Vegas. I'm literally betting her life that they took her there. If I get there and can't find her, I don't know what I'll do besides rain Hell on everyone who could've possibly been involved.

I don't have time for bureaucratic bullshit, plus I know some guys that can help me better than the feds. I run inside the corner store and grab a burner phone. They've come a long way over the years, but they're nothing like the smartphone I'm used to.

I toss the new phone in the other seat and scrub my hands over my face. The last call I need to make has my stomach turning, but I know it has to be done.

It only rings twice before it's answered.

"Brian," he says in a voice I've known and loved since birth.

"Dad," I greet him. "There's something I have to do."

"I already don't like the sound of this, son."

I give a light laugh thinking he's going to hate the details. "There's something I have to do. I can't go into much detail, but I have to go out of town for a bit, and I'm going to be unreachable for a while."

His silence is telling. I know he's weighing between being a father, albeit of a grown man, and concern for his child.

"You know my motto, Brian."

"Always do right by other people," we say in tandem.

It's his turn to laugh.

"Do what you have to do, but stay safe, son."

"Always," I tell him before hanging up.

My very last call is to the kennel. Scout is going to hate me after this, but I know she'll be well taken care of. I have another girl I need to worry about right now.

Chapter 10
Aviana

Darby is the only woman here that will give me the time of day. All of the others seem to be in competition with everyone. They all know I'm here against my will. The majority of the men that come to "visit" don't even look my way because that's not why I'm here. Yet, they still hate me and treat me as an adversary.

It may have more to do with Darby though. From what I can tell, most of the men prefer her. I've even witnessed a few of the guys argue over who was going to get to spend time with her on a particular evening. Sometimes, the argument was settled by her taking both of the guys back to her room.

Threesomes. Clearly the guys loved them, and Darby had no problem with them either. This is what angered the other women. I never thought I'd see the day where women hated other women for sleeping with a man that wasn't theirs. Today was Saturday, a busy day for the guys that came around. Darby had told me earlier in the week that Fridays and Saturdays were the quietest here.

With that information, I was bound and determined to finally get her to explain to me exactly how this whole brothel thing worked. I like to have as much information as possible about my surroundings, but more than that, I'm hoping she'll let information slip that I can use to break out of here.

We'd just gotten comfortable on one of the couches in the living area when the now familiar ding of the elevator on the other side of the steel could be heard. Seconds later the heavy, thick door swung open. *So much for it being a quiet night.*

Three handsome men, two of which I've seen here before, came strolling in. Their suits fit them perfectly, and I watched as a wicked smile came over Darby's face. She began to visibly preen and tug her tank top down, exposing more of her large breasts.

One of the guys winked at her, but he followed behind the other two down the hallway. From our vantage point on the couch, we could see them use a key card to gain access to one of the women's room. Sheila had only been here a few days, but she kept mostly to herself. The few times I did see her, she looked completely out of her head. I couldn't tell if she was baked all the time or if she had some severe disabilities.

I hear some muttering, and then the guys came out of the room. One guy was in the front, and the other two were on opposite sides of Sheila as they guided her to the door.

"Where are they taking her?" I ask softly. She shakes her head as if telling me not to talk and doesn't look my way.

Before the echo of the steel door closing dissipates, I see several women leave their rooms and go into Sheila's. A minute or so later they each come out with an arm full of her belongings.

"Fucking vultures," she mutters under her breath. "They act like the SINdicate doesn't pay for every damn thing we need."

"She won't be back?" Sheila seemed lost since the first day she got here, but that doesn't mean I don't have empathy for what's going to happen to her. For all I know I may be in the same boat soon.

"Nope," she says and shakes her head for emphasis. "I'm surprised they brought her here first."

"Where do they take them?" I ask again, hoping, this time, she'll actually answer me since the men are gone.

"The Cat House," she says.

The Cat House? Seriously?

"The guys must have hoped her being here would've helped her. They usually don't let them come back."

"She's been here before?"

"Yeah, she was here a few months ago. They took her to The Cat House. I was curious why they brought her back."

"What in the hell is The Cat House?"

She looks at me like she doesn't know if she should answer me. She darts her head around seeing if anyone else is in earshot. "The Cat House," she whispers causing me to lean in closer. "That's where they take the women when none of the guys want to visit with them here. They become street girls rather than SIN VIPs."

I gasp and bring both hands to my cheeks. "They make them become hookers?"

"Yep," she says with the P-popping on her lips. "Not exclusive like we have it here. I never want to be a street girl."

I mean, yeah, who the fuck would? Then again, I still can't fathom doing what she does either. I've done my best not to be judgey, but it pops up every once in a while.

So somewhere there is a whole group of girls that have been forced to sell themselves on the street. The women here may want that for themselves, but surely there are women at The Cat House that don't want to be in that life. I don't care if people do things, and it's by choice, but when you take away the right to choose from a woman, that's the lowest of the low.

"I've been meaning to ask you," I begin hoping the next conversation seems like an appropriate segue from the one we were just having. "How exactly does it work around here?"

She raises an eyebrow, and I watch as a little smirk comes across her face. "I was wondering when you were going to get curious enough to want the details."

I just nod my head, because I know she'll shut down if I indicate that I want to know for a different reason than what she's thinking. I can tell by the look in her eyes that she thinks I'm interested in joining the VIPs, that will never happen.

"I don't know each and every girl's struggle. Only mine." She looks around the room once more. "They've pretty much hated me since I got here, so I haven't learned much about them."

She takes a sip of water from the bottle in her hands and begins explaining the ins and outs.

"Vito found me dancing in a crappy club. The pay was terrible, and the tips were even worse. He was handsome and clean." She smiles big. "Most of the guys that showed up at the nasty place made you question whether or not you'd catch an STD from a lap dance."

I wince because that's pretty freaking bad.

"He watched me all night. I knew when I laid eyes on him the first time he sauntered through the door like he owned the place, I was going to have a piece of him." She laughs, "And by piece, I mean I was going to fuck him and roll him."

I'd like to find the comedy in this, but I've seen Vito. No way I'd ever look at him and think that I could rob him and survive.

"It didn't go as planned. He caught me of course. I'd thought I gave it to him so good he was passed out. Apparently not," she says rolling her eyes. "I gave him my sob story because I knew he could kill me if he wanted to. He had a hold of my wrists, and all I could think about was the gun he had put in the bedside table before we had sex. I just knew my life was over. I still don't know to this day if it was because of my skills in the sack or my sob story that I'm here."

"He made you come here because you tried to rob him?"

She laughs. "No he told me about this place, and I was all for it."

I stay quiet because although I find her story interesting, these aren't the details I initially asked about. She peels the label on the bottle of water in her hands, and I wonder just how much of her saying she likes it here is truth.

"Tell me about the contract." She mentioned signing a contract the first day we met, and I'm confused as to why she signed one and I didn't. Her story sounds like she had a choice, even if it was dubious.

"The contract," she begins, "lays out the bank account and what each thing we do is worth."

I tilt my head hoping she goes into much more detail, because what she's just said doesn't explain a damn thing.

She laughs at my reaction. "Okay. Each time we visit with a guy, what we do with them has a price. A blow job is a different price than sex. Three-ways and group sex carry the highest price. Anal pays the most if you're only with one guy."

You're? Is she implying me or talking about herself?

"They just give you money each time they come in?"

She shakes her head no. "They set up an account on your first day, and they make deposits in it. My contract is for five years. I've been here almost half that. When our contract expires, we can sign another one or take our money and leave."

"Are you sure they actually pay people when they leave?" I mean if they didn't, the women didn't really have a leg to stand on.

Darby had told me before we were in Vegas and I know for a fact prostitution is illegal in Clark County, not that it doesn't happen, but they wouldn't have a legal standing. I want to slap myself for sitting here like an idiot arguing over the legality of this operation when they've abducted me, and they're apparently sending other women out and forcing them into prostitution on the street.

"The only other women that have been here longer than me are still here. I have no clue how long their contracts are. The only ones that have left here are the ones that refuse to work their contract or are too fucked up to suck dick." She's so blunt, and even though what she says shocks the shit out of me, I find it refreshing.

She's told me a lot, but nothing I can really use to get out of this damn place.

"I noticed the guys use a key card and just walk into Sheila's room," I say.

"The guys have master keys. You can lock the door from the inside, but their key overrides it."

That's a scary thought. I know the doors don't lock unless we lock them from the inside. My last sense of safety in this place has just been torn from me. I know now I have to see if there's anything in the room I can use to block the door at night. I know they can come inside anytime they want, but if they have to shove furniture out of the way, it at least, gives me time to wake up.

"Fuck," I mutter. "Do they have cameras in the rooms too?"

She angles her head to the front door. "No. The only camera I've seen is the one on the other side of the door."

"Thank God for that," I say.

"You should give it a try," she coaxes me. "Vito does this thing with his tongue…"

"I'll pass," I say quickly before she can go into detail about her time spent with the man who is single-handedly holding me captive.

Besides, what man sleeps with a hooker and performs oral sex on her? Isn't that just for men who want to please the woman, rather than a sure thing he's paying her for?

Chapter 11
BT

Six hours in the air plus the one-hour layover in Dallas did nothing but give me time to run worse case scenarios through my head. I'm exhausted by the time I make it to Albuquerque and get behind the wheel of my rental car. I asked for an older model car at the crappiest car rental place I could. I'm hoping they keep shitty records, and it will be even harder for the people in Vegas to track anything back to Tampa and inevitably Aviana.

What I didn't expect was this horrible clunker which I'm not even sure will make it to Farmington. The three-hour trek across New Mexico turns into four and a half hours with how easy I have to go on the damn hunk of metal. I don't have the time to spare, but I sure as shit don't have time to be stuck in the middle of the damn desert.

It's late by the time I knock on the door of the Cerberus MC Clubhouse door. They're expecting me. I spoke with Shadow late yesterday evening and explained exactly everything I knew and what my plans were. He called me a stupid mother fucker, but I knew he was willing to help.

I know the Cerberus guys from my lengthy stay at Walter Reed in D.C. Both Blade and I were there for quite some time. These guys visited him often when they were on leave. I'm lucky to have Blade; hell the world is lucky to still have Blade. We became friends, which happens when people are trying their best to get through the worst in their lives. We've kept in touch ever since.

I knew Shadow was the man I needed to talk to when going to Vegas to track down Aviana became my plan. He's an expert in all things digital. I know I need a new identity, and he's the only guy I trust to help me out with this. Hell, he's the only guy I know with the ability to do it. I don't associate with people who do things that even border on illegality, much less this, which is felonious on so many levels.

Cerberus MC consists of all former military men. They don't talk about what they do, and I've never asked, but I know they are some sort of sub-government contract group. I know that Shadow doing this favor for me is not something he'd ever get in trouble for. I wouldn't put a friend in that situation, but man am I glad to have them.

"You mother fucker," Shadow says as he pulls the door open wider to allow me to step through.

He pulls me into a manly, back-slapping hug before releasing me and giving me a slight shove out of his personal space. Nothing better than being around like-minded men. You can smell the testosterone in the air around these guys. They're patriots, same as me, and one of the best group of men you could have the privilege to meet.

"I got you all set up, but Kincaid wanted to talk with you. You gonna hang out here for the night?" He asks as he closes the door and starts to walk deeper into the room.

"If you have a place for me to rack up and don't mind," I say. I'm completely exhausted. I was going to get a hotel room for the night and head out in the morning, but the idea of climbing back into the piece of shit car again tonight has my body hurting more than it already did.

"You're welcome as long as you need, brother." Shadow slaps me on the back. "Sorry to hear about your girl, man," he says as we head into a room with a huge oval table in the center.

"Thanks," I say because I don't want to have to explain that I'm chasing after a girl who kissed me a few times and not my actual girlfriend. I never said she was, and he assumed, so I leave it alone. Besides, these guys would laugh me out of the fucking clubhouse if I told the true story of how I was the one to put the brakes on and she was the one pushing for sex.

Her not being my girlfriend doesn't matter, and I'm certain these guys would agree. The principle fact is, a woman was abducted and is suffering through God knows what because of her piece of shit father. That's not going to be okay with any of these guys.

Kincaid stands as I make my way into the room. I reach out and shake his hand in greeting. It seems the guys were either waiting for me, or they have just finished a meeting of their own. Kincaid introduces me to the other guys around the table. I recognize Snatch, but the other guys must have never come to Walter Reed because their faces aren't familiar.

"We're just waiting on," Kincaid begins as the door to the room swings open.

"Whose fucking jalopy is that out front?" the young guy says falling down dramatically into a chair. He's in sweats and a t-shirt, both soaked from a recent workout.

Several of the guys around the table chuckle at him and shake their heads. He's young, twenty-five max. I don't know why, but I like him already.

"This is Kid, BT," Shadow says with a big smile on his face. "Have a good workout there, fella?" Shadow taunts as I reach across the table and shake hands with the man.

He sneers at Shadow but returns my handshake. Clearly there's an inside joke going on with these guys, and most days I'd be interested in hearing about it, but there's bigger shit going on for me right now.

Kincaid clears his throat and the room quiets immediately. The power this man yields in this club is outstanding. I sweep my head around the room and realize it has nothing to do with power and everything to do with respect.

"I've filled all the guys in on what you told me," Shadow says.

I nod. "Are you sure you don't need our help?" Kincaid asks.

I've spent a ton of time thinking about this, and help would be greatly appreciated, but if this shit went south, the last thing I wanted was injured or dead men on my conscious. I have enough of that shit to last a lifetime.

"It will be just a quick in and out. I can handle it." He gives me a look that says he's not buying my bullshit. "I need to do this," I emphasize.

"You want to be her hero," Kincaid counters.

I shrug because honestly that's a part of it too.

"I want to send at least one man with you." All of the guys shift their weight so they're standing taller in their seats. Short of raising their hand saying "pick me, pick me!" it's a clear sign they all want to head to Vegas with me. I cut my eyes across at Kid who seems more stuck in his own grumpy world rather than paying attention to what Kincaid is saying.

"I could use a little help," I concede. It's always nice to have a second man on the ground, especially when you're having to shovel through surveillance.

"Kid's going to be your best bet," Shadow says from beside me.

Kid jerks his head up so fast the table shakes slightly. He glares at Kincaid rather than Shadow, even though he's the one that spoke the words. The man knows the order is coming from the top.

"Don't give me that look," Kincaid chastises. "You need to get your ass out of New Mexico for a while."

"But, Khloe," he begins.

"Khloe. Exactly," Kincaid says and gives him a stern look, and true to his name and prior behavior he looks like a heartbroken child.

He grumbles but doesn't say another word.

Shadow slides an envelope in front of me. "This should be everything you need. Driver's license, prepaid MasterCard. There's ten grand on it now but let us know if you need more." I nod my head. I won't take that with me; it doesn't fit into my plan. "We have a couple of cars in the garage you can use. If they run the plates, it comes back to the guy on the license." He has a huge smirk on his face.

I realize why immediately when I pull the identification from the envelope. "Mike Hawke? Seriously?" Everyone around the table gets a good laugh at that.

Mike Hawke. *My Cock*.

"Very funny," I mutter but can't help but smile. Shadow has always had a sick sense of humor, and I love him for it.

"It's a great conversation starter," he says and slaps me on the back. "Let me show you to a room so you can get some rest."

I stand from the table and shake everyone's hands again. "Leave about eight in the morning?" I say to Kid as he stands up.

"Sure, man. It's your show," he grumbles before walking away.

I hear him mutter something about being around hookers and having no self-control as he leaves the room.

I raise an eyebrow at Shadow. "Girl trouble," he says with a smile on his face.

"Apparently," I comment back.

Chapter 12
BT

I haven't slept well in days. Last night was no exception, even though I was exhausted. The flight and the drive from Albuquerque in the piece of crap car weren't even enough to tire me out so I could sleep. I have a feeling that until this situation with Aviana is resolved, I won't get much sleep at all.

If I were going alone, I would've left last night. I fought the urge to track Kid down and hit the road. He didn't seem very happy yesterday about the idea of going to Vegas. As a matter of fact, he was the only one who didn't seem eager to tag along.

He didn't show up at dinner time when it seemed like everyone else in the MC was there. I got to meet Kincaid's girl, Emmalyn. She's probably one of the sweetest women I've ever met. I couldn't help but wonder what it would be like to find someone you just can't live without.

I date, but I've just never felt that spark with anyone… well until my lips met Aviana's for the first time. I'm not going to say it was love at first kiss, but there was something there that's never been with another woman before. I know that it's part of the reason I'm risking everything to track her down, that and the fact that she was abducted. Her abduction isn't something I could just turn a blind eye to, and I couldn't hand it over to the police and wish for the best.

I had every intention of leaving the credit card Shadow gave me on the dresser of the room I stayed in last night. Ten thousand dollars isn't much for them, and it's a drop in the bucket compared to what is owed to the SINdicate by her father, but it's a hell of a lot of money to me. An amount I'd struggle to pay back at any rate. I do know, however, that it may be necessary at some point.

I do leave behind all evidence that BT Urruela exists. I may have walked into this clubhouse as one man, but I'm leaving as Mike Hawke, even as ridiculous as the name is. I shake my head and grin as I close the door to the room and make way to the living room in search of Kid. It's time we head out; we have an eight-hour drive ahead of us today, and I plan to hit the casino as soon as we make it to town.

Laughter draws me into the kitchen where the majority of the crew from yesterday is having breakfast.

"Grab some grub," Shadow says when he notices me standing in the doorway.

I'd rather be on the road, but I know I have to eat. I grab a plate and load it up; hoping Kid eats a big breakfast as well. The fewer stops between here and Vegas the better.

I sit beside Shadow and begin to shovel food into my mouth. "In a hurry?" he asks with a chuckle.

I just nod my response.

Kid is across the room sitting beside a young girl who can't be any older than fifteen or sixteen. They have their heads down, talking to each other.

She looks incredibly young, and it makes me wonder if she's the daughter of one of the guys in the club. I'm certain they aren't keeping teenagers around this place.

The other guys all seem to be lost in conversation as well, most sidled up to one of the women I found out were "club girls." I discovered last night that the ladies that hang around the club were pretty much up for anything. I can't pull my eyes away from a redhead and the member who was introduced as Snatch yesterday. He's leaning far back in his chair, and although I can't see what she's doing, both of her hands being under the table and the glassy look in his eyes are a pretty good indicator.

Shadow's laughter makes me pull my gaze from them. "You regret the offer from last night?"

"Naw," I answer slightly embarrassed at getting caught staring at them. Shadow offered me the company of one of the club girls last night. Apparently they were pulling straws to see who got me the minute I walked in the door. Him relaying the information was strange, but I can admit that it was also flattering. Had I not been heading across the country to rescue a girl I can see staying in my life a while, I might have taken one of them up on the offer. Every one of the girls are beautiful, so it's not like it would've been a hardship.

I narrow my eyes at Kid and the girl he's sitting beside. He has his hand around her shoulder, and I'm suddenly disgusted at the idea that she may be a club girl. I can't even fathom this club doing that.

Shadow must sense my apprehension. "She's older than you think," he says from beside me.

"Eighteen?"

"Seventeen is the age of consent in New Mexico," he answers. "But he won't touch her until she's eighteen. Kincaid is sending him out with you to make sure of it. Her birthday is in a few weeks." He laughs again and gestures with his head toward the young couple. "He's going out of his mind here, and she's not helping the matter any."

The girl wraps her arms around his shoulders and leans in to kiss him on the cheek. He almost looks pained at the situation. He pecks her on the cheek and stands from the table. I don't miss the adjustment of the front of his jeans as he walks toward us.

"You ready?" he asks.

I laugh but stand from the table. "Yeah, man. Let's go."

"Thank fuck," he mutters. "I have to get away from that girl before I do something that lands me in jail."

***

The trip to Vegas wasn't as bad as I thought it was going to be. The further we got from Farmington, the better Kid's mood got. By the time we passed the "Welcome to Vegas" sign, he was one of the funniest fuckers I've ever met. I found out he was a Marine, and as much as he thought going in he wanted to make a career out of it, he realized very quickly it wasn't a long-term thing. He served one four-year enlistment and got out close to the time Shadow and Kincaid did. He served with them for one tour with Special Forces.

Special Forces is pretty elite, but the jobs he's working now seem to be a better fit for him, at least that's what he says.

Even on a Wednesday night, the Strip is packed with tourists. As much as I want the thick cut fries from Fat Burger, I drive right past to a decent hotel off the strip. We grab a couple rooms there; then head over closer to The Golden Dragon and get a room in a shitty motel within walking distance. Mike Hawke is a sad excuse of a man, down on his luck. He wouldn't have a pot to piss in much less a car to drive.

Kid is taking the car back to the nicer hotel and will grab a cab over to the casino. I sway and stagger through the front door of the casino shortly after stowing Mike's meager belongings in the motel room. I ran water in the shower and mussed up the bed to make it look like someone had been staying there. I even brought in the fast food trash from our trip and put it inside. It may be a few days before I even have to stay there, but I still need it to look lived in.

I have to keep my wits about me, so pretending to be drunk at first arriving is easier than actually drinking to get drunk once I'm here. I sit down at a blackjack table with a handful of other seedy looking guys. I'm hoping my dirty, ripped t-shirt, crappy shoes, and Walmart brand jeans are enough to convince whoever it is handing out loans that I'm desperate.

I dropped everything in Tampa and headed this way within twenty-four hours of finding Aviana's father, so there was no time to let my beard get shaggy. I had to shave it. I'm going to fuck these guys up even harder just for that. I can still taste the shaving cream and bitterness as I toss back a shot of tequila.

"Hit me," I tell the dealer on eighteen. It's a stupid fucking move, and everyone at the table knows it. I get the king the next guy would have hit twenty-one with.

"Stupid fucker," he grumbles as the dealer throws down a six on his eleven.

Ten hands later and I'm "broke" and sitting at a now empty table. My shitty hands have made everyone around me get up and find a table where people who actually know what they're doing are playing.

"Fuck," I grumble and get up from the table. I head to the teller to make a withdrawal knowing I won't have any luck there either.

I stand before the ATM for fifteen minutes, swaying back and forth, cursing it for all it's worth because it won't spit out money. I'm hoping I'm putting on a good enough show because I'm starting to feel like a schmuck.

"I can't get this to work," I slur handing the teller my card.

"How much would you like?" She asks as she swipes the card into her computer.

I laugh loudly. "How much can I get?"

She frowns at her screen. "This says you have thirteen dollars and forty-eight cents in the account."

"I'll take it!" I say with an excited slap to the counter.

"I'm sorry, sir," she says handing the card back to me. "We can't make withdrawals less than twenty plus the fee."

"Are you fucking kidding me?" I yell louder than I ever should speak to a woman. My dad would kick my ass if he saw this. She shrinks back slightly, and I feel like a total asshole now. Poor thing, it's not her fault.

She stands taller, and I can tell she's looking at someone over her shoulder. I'm hoping it's who I need and not security.

"I get paid tomorrow," I tell her for good measure.

"You should come back tomorrow," she says with more backbone that she had just the minute prior.

"Come with me, sir," I hear a gravelly voice say from behind me.

I fumble and fall into him as I turn. "Easy there," he says grabbing my upper arms to help me steady myself.

"Thanks, man," I mutter.

"You having trouble with your card?" he asks.

"Yeah. My direct deposit hasn't hit yet." He's wearing a nice suit and not a security uniform.

"I bet I can help you out." *Pay dirt.*

"That'd be great, man." For impact, I wipe my mouth on my arm like a drunken man with no money.

"Follow me," he says and turns toward a door beside the teller's station. Access to the loan shark right beside her. How convenient.

He uses a passcode to unlock the door then holds it open for me. It slaps shut behind us, and the sound reverberates off the walls sending a wash of unease down my spine.

Thirty yards down the narrow hall and a quick elevator ride into the bowels of the casino and the man in the suit steps up to a closed door. "Vinnie SINclair" is posted on a placard beside the door. Suit man knocks and gets an "It's open" from behind the door.

"Hey, boss," suit man says walking into the office. I follow him like the lost, poor puppy that I am. "This guy needs some help until his direct deposit hits tomorrow."

"Have a seat." Vinnie, I presume, is sitting behind a heavy desk in the center of the room. Just like any classic mob movie from Hollywood, he's obese, wearing an ill-fitted suit, and smoke from a cigar curls up from an overfull ashtray on his desk.

Doing as he's instructed, I flop down in the single chair that's in front of his desk. I groan in relief and allow my head to roll slightly on my shoulders.

"How much you need?" Vinnie asks.

I glance over my shoulder and see suit man near the door, looking bored with his arms crossed over his chest.

"Couple hundred," I tell him. "My check is about that much this week." I rub my hand over my bare face and immediately want to kick this fat bastard in the face. If this whole ordeal goes south, I'm certain it's because I had shaved off the beard.

"You look familiar," he says with narrowed eyes. My blood runs cold. Fuck my life if this thing is over before I can even get started. "You borrow from me before?"

Relief washes over me. "Nope. I never borrowed from anyone. It's just been a shitty year, but my luck's changing. I can feel it."

Suit man huffs a chuckle from behind me. Apparently they hear that a lot around here.

"I don't loan out a couple hundred," Vinnie says, blowing a puff of smoke in my face.

"Thank you for your time," I say and attempt to get out of the chair. In my "drunken state," it takes a few tries.

"I can do a little more," he says as suit man puts a hand on my shoulder indicating I need to stay in the chair.

"Sure, okay," I say with an over exaggerated shrug of my shoulders.

"I'm a businessman. You gotta sign a contract," Vinnie informs me.

"I'll sign anything you want if I can get back out to the tables before my luck runs out," I slur.

He pulls a stapled packet from a drawer in the desk and slides it across to me. I snatch a pen from the cup on the desk and flip to the back page.

"When do I have to pay you back?" I ask holding the pen above the signature line.

"Loans this small have to be paid in a week," he informs me.

I nod my head and sign on the line.

"You ain't gonna read that first?"

"I'm pretty sure it doesn't say you'll kill me if I can't pay," I say with a shrug of my shoulders.

They both release a menacing laugh as I slide the contract back over to Vinnie.

"Can I get a copy of that?" I ask because after that laugh any person would ask for one.

"I'll keep it safe for you right here," Vinnie says as he files my signed contract in the drawer.

"It's all yours," he says slapping a stack of bills in front of me.

The two straps on the hundred dollar bills read "Ten Thousand." I gulp a swallow and know immediately how easy it was for Aviana's father to rack up so much debt to these men.

I manage to lose every penny of the loaned twenty thousand dollars in less than two hours. I stumble out of the casino around midnight, knowing I'm either going to get lucky with this whole thing, or I'd just signed my own death warrant in the shittiest casino in Las Vegas.

Chapter 13
BT

I have a week to figure who these guys are and where they're keeping Aviana. They took a copy of my driver's license and made me fill out a form with my motel information before I left Vinnie's office. I could feel eyes on me with each staggering step I took last night on the way back to the crappy motel room.

I'd waited a few more hours inside the room to make sure whoever followed me was just verifying I'd told the truth about where I was staying. By three in the morning, I was sure they'd left to go swindle some other poor bastard who was down on his luck.

Less than five hours later and we were parked with the rear entrance to the casino in our sight. Kid stayed on a slot machine near the teller's station after he saw them take me back. He got a better look at some of the players than I did. Suit man and Vinnie were the only ones I had contact with. I suddenly realize my stupidity at thinking I could do this alone.

"I had a good look at two other guys last night that took people back," Kid says with a mouthful of breakfast sandwich.

"I can't believe I blew twenty thousand dollars. It's hard as fuck to suck that bad at blackjack," I mutter.

"What exactly is your plan?" he asks after a long swig out of his Styrofoam coffee cup.

"I'm hoping we can follow them to where Aviana is."

"And then?"

I shrug. "Then we pull her out and go back home."

"Didn't I hear you tell Shadow that they took her from Tampa?" Kid asks keeping his eye on the back of the building.

"Yeah," I said realizing what he's going to say next.

"And you think just taking her back makes it all better? That they won't come for her again?" I hate the way his laugh sounds bouncing around inside the car.

I didn't think this shit through at all.

"We have to get inside," he says more to himself.

"I," I say correcting him. "I have to get inside."

"How do we make that happen?" He asks turning his attention to me.

"I have to bait them and hope it works, I guess."

"I guess?" he says mocking me. "This poor girl. She's fucked if you're all she's got." He says it without malice, and I begin to wonder if he's right.

We watch the door for another hour in silence. Sure he's running scenarios through his head like I have been, I look over at him.

"If they come for me, and they take me, you need to let that happen," I tell him. I make my tone one that can't be argued with, but it doesn't stop this young one.

He shakes his head no. "That's not how we work, man. Kincaid would have my ass if something happened to you on my watch. I mean you're your own man, and can do whatever you want, but I'm not coming under fire with my Prez. No fucking way." He shakes his head no for emphasis.

"Well this is my plan," I begin. "Tell me if you have a better one."

***

Kid grabbed another rental car so we can watch both the back of the casino as well as the attached hotel. I'd feel more comfortable doing this recon shit with an entire team, and I'm already regretting not taking Shadow up on his offer to send more guys.

We've watched the place all week. We've followed the guys we could identify each time they've left, but they never lead us anywhere but other shitty casinos and back alleys where they meet up with men who clearly have been unable to repay their debts.

These guys are brutal, and I'm not looking forward to what I'm sure is coming for me. Climbing out of the shower this morning, my burner phone rang with an unlisted number coming across the screen. It had the Vegas, seven oh two, area code so I knew what to expect.

"Hello," I grumble into the phone.

"You got my money, Mike?"

Vinnie.

"Vinnie!" I say in an excited tone. "I'm gonna hit it big tonight. I just need a little more time."

"That right?" He says and I hear the exhale of his cigar smoke into the receiver. Even over the phone, this fucker is practically blowing smoke in my damn face.

"I feel it my bones."

"That's what you said last week before you blew your whole wad before leaving my place."

"So you got it back," I say stupidly. "We're even then right?"

"Yeah, okay, Mike. We're even." More smoke being blown into the phone. "See you soon then, see ya real soon."

The line goes dead, and I know it's go time.

***

The door to the motel shatters off of its hinge, and for a split second, I'm grateful I used an alias and paid cash for the room. I yell and rouse from what the men must assume is sleep. What else would two guys be doing in a motel room at four in the morning?

Three guys storm into the room, which surprises me. They've only been working in pairs the times we've seen them confront people. I smile inwardly, because even though I can wear shitty clothes and play the part, I can't hide my build. Muscles cover my six-foot-one-inch frame, and clearly they're anticipating a little more resistance than usual.

One guy grabs for Kid and holds him back. I know Kid could fight him off if he wanted to, but that's not part of the plan. I can tell by the look in his eyes he's not very happy with letting some guy manhandle him without resisting.

"Let go of me," he demands wrenching his shoulders slightly. "Who the fuck are you?"

The guy holding him doesn't answer. I jump off the bed and end up with my back against the wall. Not the best position to be in.

The remaining two guys head for me, and I give them my best. I catch one man on the jaw as he unsteadily comes across the bed. His feet tangle in the sheets, and crashes into the wall beside me. He hit pretty hard but not hard enough to keep him down for long.

The third guy cages me in deeper in the corner. My fist connects with his jaw. The satisfying pop makes me smile as I watch his eyes go wide. Call me a masochist, but I feed off of the energy I'm giving when his fist lands against my face. A quick jab to the stomach makes him curve around his clenching hands.

I'm about to knee him in the nose, when the guy on the ground grabs my leg and pulls it out from under me. I fall forward. With nothing to grab hold of, I crash to the ground. Both of the guys are on me before I can get back up.

I knee the first guy I hit in the nuts, and grab the second guy by his jacket as the first guy crumples to the ground holding his junk. I attempt a head-butt as I hold the guy closer by the lapels of his coat, but the hit lands off-centered to his cheek. I'm sure it's painful but not enough to keep him from fighting.

Out of the corner of my eye I see the guy holding Kid back swing him to the side. The crack I hear as Kid falls and crashes into the nightstand makes my stomach roll. I can see his feet at the end of the bed, and he doesn't move. Free of an opponent, the third man comes for me as well.

It isn't until two of the men are holding me while the third guy wraps his hands around my throat that I realize I may not have thought this through enough. Not only am I about to die, but I'm the reason Kid is lying lifeless ten feet away, possibly with a broken neck.

My vision goes blurry first, then the dark halo of oxygen deprivation darkens it completely.

"What are we going to do with the other guy?" I hear one of them ask.

"Leave him," another one answers. "He doesn't owe us anything," I hear him say before darkness takes over my world.

My last thought before I die is that I've failed Aviana, and I was her last hope.

Chapter 14
Aviana

"What the hell?" I scream sitting up suddenly in bed.

Vito is standing across the room and even in my sleep, I could feel his eyes on me. All of the furniture in the room was too heavy to move on my own, and Darby refused to help me, stating she couldn't do anything to compromise her being here.

"Seriously, Vito. What are you doing in here?"

He has a black eye, and I smile thinking that someone punched him in his handsome face.

"Only two more weeks before your father's deadline," he sneers. It's the first time he's been aggressive toward me.

As long as I've been here, no one has ever been mean, ugly or disrespectful. Until now.

The small sense of safety I've begun to feel has just been wiped away with one sentence.

A tear rolls down my cheek unbidden as I clutch the blanket to my chest.

"Don't cry, baby," he says with no hint of affection in his tone. "I can always put you on the payroll."

I know in my heart of hearts I would never be like the other women here. I may not believe in relationships, but I believe in a woman's choice. Forced into having sex with men to pay off a debt accumulated by my father is something I'd die before ever doing. Vito, however, doesn't know that.

"I don't know what you're saying," I answer, pretending as if I have no idea what the women are doing here.

"Show the guys a good time, and I'll start taking that in trade for what your father owes." He states it simply, like it's the most lucrative offer he's ever given to someone.

"I don't know," I say and hang my head. What I really want to do is tell him to go fuck himself and he might as well kill me if that's my only option. The Cat House comes to mind, and I know that death isn't the worst thing they could do to me.

"H... how long would it take to pay back?" I'm curious about the prices. Darby mentioned which things brought more money, but she wouldn't give exact prices. Curiosity has me wondering if the rates are the same for each girl or if they change them on a whim.

He laughs, and the sound makes me jerk my head up. "You'd be here a long time, Aviana. I won't lie about that." He bites his lip, and I know he's trying to look enticing, but the sight of him disgusts me. "But

I get the feeling the guys are going to love you, so it'll go by faster than it would with most girls."

I give him a weak smile while trying to swallow back the bile that's slowly climbing the back of my throat. For the first time since I got here, I feel hopeless. I make a mental note to find a weapon to keep in my room. I can use it to fight off anyone who comes in here, or if worse comes to worse, I can use it to take care of myself.

"Give it some thought, baby." I hate the way the term of endearment sounds coming out of his mouth. "I could be your first. I'd break you in real good."

I keep my head down as he opens the door to leave.

"I tip really well, too," he says before leaving the room and closing the door softly behind him.

No one seems to be willing to tell me the ins and outs of the "business" they're running here. With Darby, I honestly think she doesn't know but is too embarrassed to admit she's not sure what she's making by sleeping with the guys and doing God knows what else.

Vito isn't going to give me any information either. I'm being held captive here, and even more of a threat than the other women who are here willingly. I did hear Darby mention that the drugs they bring in are not free. Those are deducted from the money the women are making.

It's a vicious cycle. The women get high to sleep with the men to earn money. Yet, they snort all of the "profit" they're making whoring themselves out. I heard one of the other girls talking in the kitchen last night that Sheila was taking more up her nose than she was making with the men, and since there was no return on investment any longer with the SINdicate, they removed her.

I'm afraid I'll meet the same fate.

***

The longer I stay in my room, the more my mind races with the proposition Vito spoke to me about. Knowing I have less than two weeks to get out of here before my father's deadline has me hustling out of my room in search of Darby. She has to know more. She can't have lived here more than two years and not know something. She's not one of the girls that's snorting her weight in coke.

I knock on her cracked-open door and stick my head inside.

"Hey," I say when she tells her visitor to 'come in.' "Look at you. Hot date?" I'm being sarcastic because no one ever leaves here.

This isn't the first time I've seen her show more effort for a visit from one of the guys, but it is the first time I've seen her with her hair twisted up and glamourous. My eyes falter on a gorgeous silk gown hanging from the wardrobe.

"As a matter of fact," she says applying mascara, "I do."

"What do you mean? You get to leave here?" My heart picks up, and my pulse beats loudly in my ears.

"There is a casino opening tonight. Frankie is taking me." She shrugs as if it's no big deal. To her it may not be; to me, it's a way to get out of this place.

My mind reminds me of all the things I would have to do before they'd ever allow me to step foot out of this place.

I cringe at the idea, unsure at this point if surviving would be worth it. What do I have to go home to anyway? The only thing that is back home is my crappy apartment, a shitty job, and classes that I despise.

BT. BT is back in Tampa. He's been filling my mind more often the last couple of days. I've wondered more times than I can count if he's worried about me or even noticed that I'm gone.

"You get to go out often?" I ask hoping her answer is yes.

"Not too often. A couple times a year maybe. I get to go out more than the other girls," she says with a wink.

I know the other women hate her because of her popularity with the men, but I find her self-esteem refreshing.

I laugh at her carefree attitude concerning the other women. "So, how do I score a date out of this place?" I waggle my eyebrows at her.

She pulls the mascara wand away from her face and laughs. "Lots and lots of blowjobs!"

I crinkle my nose at her. I know she's right, but cold day in hell and all that.

"How about," I proposition her, "you suck the dicks and pass the date to me."

She scoffs. "It doesn't work that way, babe."

My face falls even though I know it's not a possibility. I know they'll never let me out of here. *Unless it's to The Cat House.*

"You don't think your dad will pay?" She keeps her voice low because along with the cattiness from the other girls has come a distaste for me as well. We both know we can't trust any of the women with some of the conversations we have.

I shake my head no. "He doesn't have that type of money at all. Last time I talked to him, he was homeless. If he had two hundred thousand dollars he'd gamble it away or shoot it up his arm."

She sits beside me on the bed as a tear rolls down my cheek. "You can always work," she says softly. She's being sincere and not trying to entice me, rather she's offering me a way out. The only other choice I've been given.

I chuckle at the absurdity of it. "You sound like Vito."

"We all have to do what we need to survive, Avi."

I nod as she gives my shoulders a final squeeze and walks over to the dress hanging on the wardrobe door. She shrugs off her robe and slides the soft silky dress down her body.

"Zip me up?" she asks with her back to me.

I stand from the bed and tug her zipper up. She looks positively gorgeous. I can't help but think of Julia Roberts in *Pretty Woman*.

"Think about it," she whispers over her shoulder.

"I'll consider it," I lie.

The door swings open wider, and a handsome man in a tuxedo walks in.

"You ready?" He asks Darby before his eyes land on me.

He saunters toward me with a stride that says he's well aware of his good looks and the effect it has on women.

"Frankie," he purrs holding his hand out for me to shake. I give him my hand and he raises it to his lips. I could vomit at his charm. "Fuck, Vito was right about you. Stunning," he whispers not letting go of my hand but taking a step back to snake his eyes from my head to my toes.

I pull my hand from his. I'm in sweats and a baggy t-shirt. This guy is one hundred percent full of shit. These clothes and a few outfits like it are all that were in the room when I got here. I haven't asked for anything else because I know at the end of the day nothing is free.

"Nice to meet you," I tell Frankie politely before skirting around him and going back to my room. I stay locked in there for the rest of the night. With Darby not here, I don't feel as safe from the other women as I did before.

Chapter 15
BT

There is nothing better than waking up from a situation you thought would kill you. This isn't the first time. I squeeze my eyes together not knowing what the damage to my body is this time around. I feel like I got hit by a truck, but that's still ten times better than I felt the day I woke up from the IED explosion.

My face is swollen, and every joint in my body is tight. No doubt those fuckers continued to beat the shit out of me when I passed out. I shouldn't expect any less. I've seen how they treat people on the street. What I'm not sure about is why they left me alive. They know I can't pay back the money.

I pray that the information Shadow set up hasn't been breached. I would die if something happened to my family.

"He's waking up," I hear from my right.

I try to move and turn to the sound in an effort to defend myself if they try to pull any more sneaky shit. I realize then that my hands are tied behind my back, and my legs are tied to the chair I'm sitting in. I rotate my jaw and even though it's sore as hell I can tell it's not broken. I once again miss my beard.

I open my eyes as best I can and see one of the guys from the hotel room staring back at me. I shift my weight to lunge at him, but my restraints hold. He raises an eyebrow at me, and I see his lip twitch. Fucker thinks this shit is funny. I, personally, don't see anything about this comical, but as always it's about perception.

"This guy's like a pit bull," another guy says.

"More like a Chihuahua," the guy I'm looking at says. "Those tiny bastards don't know when to give up because they're outnumbered."

My lip twitches and they're both right. I've never felt so caged and animalistic in my life. These low life scumbags are getting off on this shit. I vow then and there if I'm given the chance I'll wipe their shit-eating grins off their faces before it's all said and done.

I twist my wrists again and feel either rope or flex cuffs cutting into my skin. My head throbs from the punches they landed on my face. A deep breath tells me a few ribs are either bruised severely or broken, and it makes me hate these guys even more.

Worst, though, is the disappointment I feel in myself for not thinking this plan through. I should've taken Kincaid up on his offer to send his entire team, but no, I had to be her hero. My failure now makes me her executioner.

I hear a door behind me open, and I can't help but wonder if they will just shoot me in the back of the head like a coward. The smell of awful cigar smoke fills my nostrils, and I know it's Vinnie before he even comes around and stands in front of me.

I guessed wrong with the thought that the big boss man wouldn't show up for the dirty part of business. Here he is in all his rotund glory. I'm almost certain we're in the casino basement, more than likely near Vinnie's office. He's slightly out of breath from the trip getting here, but not so out of breath that he's walked clear across the casino from his office.

"You owe me money," he says, blowing smoke in my face.

I turn my head to avoid catching most of it in my eyes and nose. The last thing I need is to have a coughing fit. That would surely make me look like a pussy.

"I get paid tomorrow," I lie.

He laughs, and it's the same cold, calculating laugh I heard on the phone last night before they busted into the motel room.

"No sense in lying Mr. Hawke. Did you think we'd loan you twenty thousand dollars and not run your background?"

My blood runs cold. I think about my dad, brother, and even my mom who I haven't spoken to in years. If this situation gets anymore fucked and they do something to my family, I'll either kill every one of them the second I get a chance, or I'll haunt them every second of eternity from the grave.

"We know for a fact that you lost your job last month," Vinnie says as if he's disclosing some secret I tried to keep hidden.

I release a shuttering breath. Shadow is an expert at alternate identities, and I never should've doubted him.

"I just need more time," I tell him. "Seriously, Vinnie. I can feel it in my bones. I know the big break is coming."

"More time?" He scoffs. "I could give you years, Mr. Hawke, but you don't have the money to place the next bet much less the ability to pay me back."

"So this is where you kill me?"

I watch him shrug as if ending a man's life over money is a decision he makes every day and has no issues with signing the death certificate.

"We know you have no family. Your parents died when you were young. Your wife killed herself three years ago. You have nothing left to go home to."

Fucking Shadow. I guess on paper Mike Hawke was at the lowest point of his life, but shit, he killed off my imaginary wife. I pray that doesn't end up as a premonition rather than a way to keep Mike Hawke's business right here in Vegas, dependent on one man, rather than sending these thugs to go hurt someone in an attempt to get me to comply with repayment.

"Your life sucks, man," the guy standing to my left says.

I nod in agreement, because on paper that was one hundred percent the truth. Mike Hawke's life was horrible. I hope they don't decide to make me a mercy killing. That's not exactly conducive to my plans to rescue Aviana.

As stupid as it sounds, I wonder what Batman would do in a situation like this. My favorite superhero is human, just like I am. He's selfless in his bid to rid his world of evil. Unfortunately, unlike Batman, I don't have tricks up my fucking sleeves to get out of this mess.

"You put on quite a performance last night." I look up at Vinnie as he stubs his cigar out on the concrete wall. "Vito here," he points to the man to my right that called me a Chihuahua. I smirk again at the cut on his lip. "He said you put a good fight. Not much impresses Vito these days."

I don't know how to take the compliment.

"Still ended up here, tied to this fucking chair," I mumble.

Vito laughs and cracks his knuckles. *Yeah, fucker I got you. One on one and let's see how long you keep that smile on your damn face.*

"Where did you learn to fight like that?" Vinnie asks. "Your background doesn't show anything that would indicate formal training."

"Taebo," I mutter. Vito laughs again, but the sarcasm is lost on Vinnie. Old, fat fucker wouldn't know exercise if it took a chunk out of his big ass. He raises an eyebrow at me. "I grew up in a shitty neighborhood. It was either learn to fight or get your ass whipped every day."

"You owe me twenty thousand dollars," Vinnie says, reminding me of just how fucked I am. "You know what happens to the guys that can't pay me back my money?"

I want to tell him that I heard abducting innocent women was his thing, but I keep that shit to myself. Aviana, hopefully, is still alive out there somewhere, and it wouldn't bode well for her if I mentioned anything like that.

"Besides the spa treatment I'm getting right now?" Vito and the other man in the room chuckle, but Vinnie is less than impressed. I'm a smartass, been this way my entire life. Pretty sad when I can't even turn it off in the face of adversity. This man made his mind up before he walked into this room what my fate would be. I don't imagine busting his chops a little is going to change that, and I refuse to look like a pussy. That's BT coming out; Mike Hawke would beg for his life, but at this moment in time, if I'm going to die, I'll do it with pride and dignity.

"Most men are disposed of quickly when I don't see an alternative for payment," Vinnie says. "You, however, have a certain skill set I see as being beneficial to my organization."

I tilt my head as hope flares in my chest. I don't say a word, rather I just stare at him and try to determine where he's going next.

"I have a proposition for you, Mr. Hawke," he says and narrows his eyes when he can tell I'm about to come back with some smart-assed comment. I swallow my remark and do my best to skill my face into impassivity. "I have a way to allow you to live and pay me back."

This could be worse than death. I know whatever he expects me to do will not border on legality but will cross the line so far I'll end up in prison. I nod my head, even though it's the last thing I want to do. I may only be changing the date on my death certificate, but it's better than coming to an end today.

"Whatever you need," I say, sliding back into Mike Hawke's persona.

"I'm always looking for men with your skill set." When I tilt my head in confusion, he continues. "Recovery." He says simply.

"Recovery?" I know what he's talking about, but I want him to say the words.

"You'll work with Vito here," he nods toward the guy to my right.

"A job?" I smile at him. This situation just took one hell of a turn for the better.

"Vito will show you the ropes. You can count half of what you recover toward your debt." He walks away, and I hear the door slam behind me.

This is the most ridiculous thing I've ever heard. A Vegas mob boss just loans out money like it's no big fucking deal, then offers me a job. He's so narcissistic; he doesn't even consider I'd agree and take off the first second I get a chance? Insane, the man is insane. Well, his mental health issues are only concerning to me in that he's just given me the perfect in to this organization. This is the best possible outcome I could hope for with the way the situation turned to shit.

He didn't even wait for my answer. He didn't have to; he knew I had no other choice but to say yes.

Chapter 16
BT

I shift my body quickly towards the guy I kneed in the balls earlier as he bends down to cut my legs free. I smirk when he shifts backward quickly. Clearly this fucker is scared of me. He better be. I turn my attention to Vito, who is clearly the next top guy just under Vinnie.

"We have the best resources in tracking people," Vito says before giving the guy at my feet the nod to cut my arms free. "You take off, and we'll track you down like a dog and slaughter you in the street."

Ballsy threat. "As you heard," I say calmly. "I got fired from my job. This offer is the best one I've had in years."

He nods, taking me at my word and whatever info he gathered from my background check. This actually makes him an idiot. He knows I have nothing to lose. He's well aware, according to the information they revealed, I have no family or anyone else they can torture and threaten me with like they are doing with Aviana's dad. I'm a loose cannon; a ticking time bomb at best. How these guys are too stupid to realize that I have no idea.

"Follow me," Vito says walking out of the small room.

"Where are we going?" I ask as I rub the tender area around my wrists. The skin's not broken, but angry whelp marks cover a solid one inch.

I look to my left and see the door to Vinnie's office. Right next door? The way that fucker was huffing and puffing, I was sure he, at least, took a flight of stairs. His ass won't last much longer if twenty yards has him puffing like an asthmatic teen who'd just seen tits for the first time.

"To work," Vito says hitting the up button on the elevator panel. And just like that, I became the newest enforcer for the SINdicate.

As stealthily as I can, I pat my pockets. My cell phone and wallet are gone. I have no way to reach out to the guys in New Mexico to let them know about Kid.

"What happened to the guy in the room with me?" I ask Vito, not sure if I even want what I'm assuming is tragic news. I can still hear the echo of his head hitting the bedside table in my head.

"We left his ass there," the other guy with us said.

"Alive?" I ask.

"What's it to you?" Vito sneers. "He your boyfriend or something?"

"Why?" I sneer. "You wanna take me for a spin?"

His eyes widen as if homosexuality is the grossest thing he could imagine himself doing. I'm not gay by any stretch of the imagination, but I despise people who are homophobic. Too much bigger shit going on in the world than to worry about who loves who.

"Calm the fuck down," I say doing my best to hide my annoyance. "I just met his ass last week." *Truth.* "We were sharing a room to save on costs." *Lie.*

"I just don't need the police looking for my ass when they find a fucking dead body in a room rented in my name." The thought that there may be some truth to that makes my skin crawl.

"Relax, asshole," the guy behind me says with a shove to my back. "He was moaning and groaning when we left the room. He probably has one hell of a headache, but he was alive."

Relief washes over me. I pray he doesn't interfere with the SINdicate now that I have a way inside. I told him to leave me alone if they took me, and I pray he heeds my instructions.

I have no doubt that Kincaid will send some people to keep an eye on me. No way will he just let me get grabbed up and, at least, make sure I'm okay. I take solace in knowing that they are out there, even if I can't see them or have any idea what they plan on doing. My only concern right now is to find out where Aviana is and get her ass out of Vegas.

***

"My Cock, huh?" *Mike Hawke.* Vito says with a laugh as we walk down the dark alleyway. Most people come to Vegas and have no idea about the seedy, disgusting side of the town. All they see are the lights, shows, and well-kept casinos. They don't see the crime, disease, and filth that is mere blocks away from the glamour and fun. How could they expect anything less in a city where pretty much anything goes and men have been literally getting away with murder since the first fight over land in the desert over a hundred years ago?

"My parents were assholes," I say in response to his jab at my name. The words taste like shit in my mouth. Maybe a guy named Mike Hawke's parents would be assholes. My pop, on the other hand, is one of the greatest men I'll ever know. I have to remember that Mike's life is now mine. I'm no longer BT Urruela; I'm now an indentured servant to the SINdicate.

"That guy," Vito says pointing at a man who's passed out beside the dumpster.

The man doesn't look homeless, or if he is, it's a recent event. No doubt if he's lost everything, it's because of a bet he'd made drunk with SINdicate, much like the way they got me.

"The bum?" I ask looking at the poor guy. "He wouldn't have shit on him. He'd be in a hotel sleeping it off rather than on top of a pile of garbage."

"These guys don't waste money on luxury shit like that. Gets in the way of gambling and dope." The other guy says beside me.

"Frankie's right. Check his pockets. If he gives you any trouble, punch him in the fucking mouth." Vito tilts his head toward the guy who remains passed out and oblivious to what's about to happen.

I roll my shoulders and walk up to the man. Crouching down beside him I pat his pockets. "If I get stabbed with a used fucking needle," I threaten as I reach into his pocket.

My fingers hit a roll, and my eyes go wide. Pulling the wad of cash from his pocket, I stare at the money. I grin up at Vito. "This may be easier than I thought."

"Not so fast," he says taking the cash from my hand. I watch as he pops the rubber band on the money. The twenty on the outside is protecting a roll of nothing but ones. "Less than a hundred here."

Most people would put their larger bills on the inside of their money to make it look like they have less than they do. This idiot has done the complete opposite.

"Just look at it this way," Vito says counting the money. "You're debt just decreased by forty-two bucks."

Frankie laughs, and it pisses me off so bad I want to kick the still sleeping guy on the ground.

"Come on," Vito says stuffing the meager cash into his pocket. "We got a few more before the night ends."

I follow him out of the alley just to walk a few blocks and take care of a few more guys. After the fourth guy, I'm pretty certain we're just robbing people, and it sits heavy in my stomach. I constantly remind myself this is only a means to an end, but that was harder to swallow when the last guy fought back, and I was forced to pop him in the nose to relieve him of the thirty-eight dollars he had in his pocket.

"If I keep doing this," I tell Vito wiping the vagrant's blood off of my knuckles and onto my jeans, "I'm going to need some fucking gloves. I don't want to walk away from this fucking job with AIDS or some shit."

Both he and Frankie laugh at me as we walk back to the car. Frankie drives us back to the casino, and I follow them into the attached hotel. It's only ten to twelve stories high, but the reception area is cleaner than I would've expected from the condition of the attached casino.

A short elevator ride, which required a key card Vito produced from his wallet, takes us to the tenth floor. Vito stops in front of a room and uses the same keycard to open it up. "This is where you will stay while you're working off the money you owe," he says stepping inside and flipping on the light.

The room is musty and hasn't seen a renovation since probably the seventies. I can tell by just a quick look at the bed that I was probably more comfortable when I was in the desert. I guess I should be thankful they're not keeping me in that dank room beside Vinnie's office tied to a chair.

"Thanks, man," I say with as much appreciation as I can muster.

"It's not the best, but it could be worse," Frankie says from the doorway.

"I'm not going to complain about a free room."

They both laugh again as Vito turns to leave the room. "It's not free Mr. Cock." He pats his pocket where the money is that I pulled off the men is stashed. "You almost made enough tonight to clear the cost of the room."

The door closes with a resounding thud as I realize I now owe more than the twenty thousand I was swindled into borrowing. Fuck. My. Life.

Chapter 17
Aviana

Twelve days. That's how long Vito says I have until my dad's extension is over. Less than two weeks and my borrowed time is over. I'm no closer to finding a way out of here than I was over a week ago when I arrived. Since Darby went to the casino opening thing with that guy Frankie, the other women have been even less welcoming. Catty to the point that when I enter a room, they pick their things up and leave.

I speak or say hello and they literally don't even acknowledge my existence. It's like seventh-grade year before my boobs came in all over again. You'd think grown women would be different than teenagers, but they're not. I guess I should just be glad they ignore me rather than being aggressive. Small blessings; I guess I should count every one I get.

Darby only had a few books in her room, but I borrowed The Collector by John Fowles from her. Unaware of what it was about, I thought I'd give it a try. Turns out it's about a girl getting abducted; her captor hoping she'll fall in love with him. Needless to say, I didn't get very far in it because it resonates and hits way too close to home with my situation right now. So it lies deserted on the bedside table.

I've yet to return the book to Darby because I've been distancing myself from everyone. I'm certain a doctor would diagnose me with depression at this point, but seriously, who wouldn't be depressed dealing with the shitty hand my life has been dealt recently?

Darby has also seemed a little distant herself since her date. I want to ask her if she's okay, but I'm not certain she'd want to talk to me about whatever happened while she was gone. I don't know that I'd consider Darby a friend since I'm stuck in this situation, but the longer I go without seeing if she's alright, the more guilt I feel over the entire situation.

I climb off my bed and head out toward her room. Rather than making it all the way to her room, I notice her sitting on the couch staring blankly at the TV, which is on mute.

"Hey," I say sitting down on the cushion beside her.

"Hey," she says in a less than Darby manner.

She sits silently with her eyes focused on the TV screen. I watch the muted TV for a while before speaking up.

"Are you okay?" I ask softly.

She frowns. "I don't know." It's an honest answer, I can tell. What I'm not sure of is if she wants to talk to me about what's going on.

I decide to push a bit, the worst thing she can do is tell me to fuck off.

"Did something happen on your date with Frankie?"

She huffs. "It wasn't a date. He made sure everyone knew that." She shakes her head in disappointment. "He let anyone who asked that I was pretty much a paid escort."

I wince. It may be her job, but the exclusivity of this place somewhat protects the girls here since they only interact with the guys from the SINdicate.

"Asshole," I mutter in her defense.

"And to top it off," she continues, "He had me do a gangbang with some of the other guys. Now Vito is pissed at me, and he's the best tipper."

I reach for her hand and hold it without saying a word. I have no clue what to say in a situation like this.

"Most days are fine, but since that night, I can't help but wonder if I'd be okay if I wasn't here." She sighs and drops her chin to her chest.

"Can you leave?"

She shakes her head no. "I have to fulfill my contract. If I try to leave there's no telling what will happen to me." With that information right there, I know these women are just as much captives as I am.

"And you can't turn them down because you won't meet the requirements of the contract," I say absently.

She huffs a weak laugh. "I have no problem whatsoever with the sex. That's the best part. Honestly, all of the sex is no different than life would be outside of the SINdicate."

I tilt my head at her. She mentioned she was a stripper when Vito found her but never hinted that she was a hooker before coming here.

"I'm pretty much a nympho," she admits with a smile. "I love the sex. All kinds, all the time. It's being stuck in this building day in and day out that drives me crazy the most."

I nod because I'm in the same mindset. I hate not being able to leave and at least, feel the breeze on my face, or run down to the store for a diet soda.

We chat for a little bit longer, and she seems to be in better spirits when I leave her on the couch to go to bed. I hope things begin to look up for her. I seriously miss having someone to talk to, and two depressed people talking to each other is a recipe for disaster.

***

The scratch of BT's beard on my chin and cheeks is the sexiest thing I've felt in months. The rumble of his chest and the feel of his smiling upturned lips against the soft flesh of my stomach has me writhing under him. I moan softly when his hot tongue flicks my belly button and the sensitive skin just below it.

I'm in heaven. When I reached out to grip him through his jeans as we kissed, I fully expected him to push my hand away. A faint memory told me as I reached for him that he wouldn't let this get any further than kissing. I must have broken down a barrier at some point because the feel of his hard, thick cock in my hand was heavenly.

He lifts his head slightly to smile at me, and I feel the cold metal of his dog tags tickle the swollen flesh at the apex of my thighs. The whisper soft touch is gone quickly only to be replaced with a skilled tongue and moving lips. I never knew I could enjoy teeth until BT bites my hardened clit and lashes at it with his tongue.

Gripping the sheets in my clenched fists, I'm certain I'll tear them before long. The growl in his throat as I rotate my core against his working mouth tells me he probably wouldn't mind if I rip them to shreds. With hands on the backs of my hips, he pushes my legs up higher and settles his full body on the bed, as if he plans to stay there a while. Fuck, at this point I hope he's packed a bag and plans to move in.

Jesus, the scratch of that beard against my most sensitive flesh unravels me. Instinct is that I need to be quiet, but the assault I'm under makes it impossible. I release my death grip on the sheets and reach for his ruffled hair instead. The pleasure he's giving me is so intense it's borderline painful. I fist a clump of his hair and grind my hips harder against his mouth. He takes it in stride, licking and sucking on every inch of flesh his mouth and tongue can reach.

The orgasm of my lifetime begins at the base of my spine and low in my belly. The explosion from my climax has my back arching off of the bed and my eyelids fluttering. I'm liquid as I come down from my high. I crack an eye open as I feel him move on the bed.

"Fuck, you're beautiful," he husks as he moves up my body.

I watch as he lines himself up at my center. "Are you ready for me?" He asks on a groan as he pushes the first bare inch inside of me.

Before I can answer with a resounding yes, he slams inside of me to the hilt.

I cry out. Sitting up in bed, confusion hitting me immediately as the room I'm forced to stay in comes into focus, and the dream of BT fades away. Just how my life would go, having the orgasm of a lifetime while sleeping instead of enjoying the real thing. My body still hums from what he was able to do to me while I dreamed.

Chapter 18
BT

"You were holding out on me Shane," I tell the half-naked man as I pull another wad of cash from his back pocket.

The first night with Vito and Frankie was the only night they had me trolling for bums in the back alleys. I'm thinking they were trying to see if I'd actually participate. I must have passed with flying colors because the next night they had me busting down motel doors, much like they did to mine after the phone call with Vinnie.

It's only taken a few nights of working with these guys to realize the way they operate. They're preying on weak men; men who are so down on their luck they have no way of ever getting back on top. If they were even at the top at some point in their life.

Vito never tells me what each person owes; he just pockets every single penny we pull off of each guy. The motels have also disclosed that not only are these guys getting loans in cash from Vinnie, but there is also a narcotic element to their business. That, of course, is speculation since neither Vito nor Frankie will tell me one fucking detail about the organization. I'm just their muscle, a way to keep them from having to get their hands dirty or break out into a sweat.

I shove Shane back down on the bed. He's so fucking high I don't think he realizes completely what's going on.

I hand the money to Vito and watch as he counts it. The amount really doesn't matter; it's not like I'm going to be working here to pay all the money off.

"Where to next, boss?" I follow Frankie out of the room.

"Crazy thing, Cock." Yeah, they've both been calling me that. I remind myself to punch Shadow in the nose the next time I see his ass. "The last guy on our list is just a few doors down."

We walk up a creaky flight of stairs and Frankie points to another door. The awesome thing about the motels and their occupants is that they are so old school they have actual keys to lock them and nine times out of ten the people inside are so drunk or high they don't lock the doors. I check the doorknob and BINGO, unlocked. I shove the door open and shake my head when I see the guy inside with his head bent over a mirror covered in lines of coke. Expensive habit for a guy who's borrowed money from Vinnie and his crew.

"What the fuck?" He yells but doesn't release the rolled up bill in his hand. The white residue on his nostrils clearly indicates he's been going at it a while.

I walk up and snatch the rolled up money out of his hand. Every penny counts right?

Just as I'm pulling him to his feet to check his pockets, I hear Vito say, "Jackpot!"

I look over at him and see him holding a duffle bag open. It is practically stuffed to the top with strapped up cash. I drop the guy back down and don't even care that he's practically slumped on the disgusting couch.

"That's fucking mine!" He screams again. I look back at him. I can't help but think he looks like the still-shot of a bank robber I saw on TV a few nights ago. This is fucking ridiculous.

"Only in Vegas," I mutter as Vito zips up the bag and heads to the door.

I follow him out, and once we're back in the car, I finally speak. "Half of that goes toward what I owe right?" From the looks of the amount of cash in that bag, it's enough for them to cut me loose.

"That guy owed two grand. So, a thousand of this goes towards what you owe," Frankie interrupts.

I hope the relief I feel doesn't show. The last thing I need is to be turned loose before I find Aviana, but at the rate I'm going with these guys, I'm beginning to lose hope.

After driving in silence for a few minutes, Vito finally speaks up. "Let's go get some pussy."

"Hell yeah," Frankie says. I see Vito sneer at him and wonder just what that pissed off look is about. It seems Frankie is grating on his nerves, and their already less than stellar working relationship is even more strained.

"I'm here to work," I tell Vito. "I don't have time to waste hunting down and trying to find a chick to fuck." Sex is the last thing on my mind, but worse yet is being put in a situation where they expect me to fuck some random girl as a means to prove my forced loyalty to the SINdicate.

"There's always time to worry about pussy," Frankie says with a quick laugh.

"I got just the place, Cock," Vito says with a huge smile. "Full of an array of women guaranteed to be a sure thing."

Jesus, we're going to a whore house.

Confusion washes over me as we pull up to the valet in front of The Golden Dragon. "Here?" I mutter.

"One stop shop," Vito says slapping me on the back as Frankie hands the keys to the car over to the valet attendant.

We head to the elevator, and Vito pulls out the magical key card that gets him in everywhere and inserts it into the slot provided in the wall.

"When can I get one of those cards?" I tease him, knowing 'never' will be the answer.

He winks at me. "When you're clear of your debt," he says and in my mind, it translates to 'never you stupid fucker.'

Vito hits the button for the top floor, and I inwardly groan about the stupid shit that may go on up here as we ride all the way up. I just want to find Aviana and get my ass out of the city. Just thinking of grabbing her and running makes my skin crawl. There is so much other shit going on with these guys, it's hard for me to turn a blind eye to it.

I'm not a fool; I know this shit goes on all over the world, but her safety is my number one priority. If she's safe, then I can live with the guilt of leaving behind all the other injustices going on in this city. I am but one man, I remind myself.

The elevator opens with a muffled ding, and we're standing in a small vestibule with nothing but a huge steel door in front of us. Vito puts the first key card back in his pocket and pulls out a red one stamped with The Golden Dragon's emblem on the front. He slides it into the slot and the locking mechanism whirls. The door makes a double beeping sound and opens.

Vito pauses before I can cross the threshold and I almost walk into his back.

"This pussy isn't free," he begins to explain while walking forward again. "If you fuck one of these girls, it comes out of what you earned tonight."

Fat chance of having to worry about that fucker. We step into the room and wait for the door to close behind us. I look back at it and realize without a key card like the one Vito is shoving back into his wallet, there's no way out.

I let my eyes scan the room and can tell instantly that they've just converted the hotel hallway into sort of a living room area. There are rooms to the left and right down long hallways.

I see a flash of blonde and turn to look in the direction of the movement and my eyes land on the beautiful face of Aviana. Her eyes widen, and I shake my head slightly, hoping she understands not to give anything away.

"I want that one," I say pointing directly at her.

Chapter 19
Aviana

I guess as far as being a captive goes, this place isn't so bad. There's food, the beds are somewhat comfortable, and although there are no premium channels, we at least have basic cable. Who am I kidding? This is better than how I was living back in Tampa. My apartment was in a horrible part of town, and basic cable was a dream rather than a reality there.

Darby and I are sitting on the couch making our way through a Kardashian marathon when I hear the double beep of the front door. Darby perks up, but I watch as her face falls when Vito steps through the door.

"This pussy isn't free. If you fuck one of these girls, it comes out of what you earned tonight," he explains to someone standing behind him.

My blood runs cold when the knowledge that a 'new guy' is coming in. I pray Vito has issued the warning I'm certain has been given to the other guys. That's the only reason why they've stayed away from me and don't bother me too much. Every once in a while one of the guys will make comments or try to 'persuade' me to take them back to my room, but they back off when I tell them no.

My eyes almost bug out of my head when I see no other than BT-fucking-Urruela walk through the door. I'm saddened immediately upon seeing him when Vito's words and his face makes me realize that this man is much like my father. Even worse, if he's working for the SINdicate. I'm not going to pretend I know BT even a little bit, but I never expected this.

Just before I say something I see him make eye contact with me. A quick shake of his head tells me to keep my mouth shut, and I'm hoping the way I've perceived the situation is not what it actually is.

"I want that one," he says to Vito pointing directly at me.

Vito smiles but shakes his head when he realizes who BT just pointed at. "She's off-limits, Cock."

I see relief flash across his face. Hopefully he doesn't think I've been here for a week plus having sex with the male members of the SINdicate.

"What do you mean I can't have her?" BT questions him. "You said an array of pussy guaranteed to be a sure thing."

"She's not active just yet," Frankie says as he grabs a brunette by the hand and they disappear down the hallway.

I stand from the couch. "I'll do it," I tell Vito. He raises an eyebrow at me, clearly shocked by my acceptance of the situation. I give him a casual shrug of my shoulder. "I have to start paying it back at some point, right?"

A huge smile splits Vito's face as he slaps BT on his back. "Looks like you get the maiden SINdicate voyage on sweet Avi."

I watch as BT sneers at Vito, but he masks it quickly. I watch as Vito angles his head at Darby. She pops off the couch like she's won a trip to Disneyland and saunters up to him. He jerks her arm apparently not feeling the excitement she's displaying.

I watch as they walk away. "Have fun, Cock," Vito says over his shoulder. "You only got an hour or so." They disappear behind Darby's closing door.

I reach out and take his hand, pulling him to my room.

I close us into my room and before he can open his mouth to explain just what the fuck he's doing here, I jump in his arms. I'm crying and sobbing against his chest as he holds me tight. His calming arms around me and his whispered voice soothes me immediately.

"Fuck," he whispers with his lips against my forehead. "I was afraid I'd never see you again."

Long minutes go by before I'm able to speak, and he's patient with me. Not once does he grill me about what's going on or judge me.

"What are you doing here?" I ask my voice still cracking from my sobs.

He tilts my head back and looks in my eyes. "I'm here for you, Aviana." He releases his hold on me and takes my hand. "Come on," he says tugging me to the door.

"Wait," I say and plant my feet.

"Wait?" He asks, clearly confused. "I need to get you out of here. Security is limited right now."

"Do you have one of the cards?" I ask, hopeful. He shakes his head, and I frown. "We can't get out of here without one."

"I'll go snap Vito's neck if I have to and use his," he says as if killing someone to rescue me is as simple as picking which jeans you want to wear for the day.

"What about the other girls?" I ask. Darby is in the room with Vito, and she may have wanted to leave yesterday when she thought Vito was done with her, but that may have changed now that he's back in there with her now.

"We can grab them when we leave," he says placing his hand on the doorknob again.

"You don't understand, BT. They take girls from here and put them in a place they call The Cat House. They make those women into prostitutes, forcing them to sell themselves on the street." I explain.

"Fuck," he mutters and rubs his hand over his hairless face. I almost didn't recognize him when I first saw him. It was the magnificent brown eyes I've been dreaming about that looked back at me and I knew him instantly.

I pull him by the hand and sit down on the bed, smiling lightly as he sits beside me.

"How are you even here?" I ask.

He clears his throat before he begins to speak. "You were gone for days. No class. No answer to the dozens of text messages. I was losing my shit. I figured out where you lived." He looks off into the distance for a brief second. "Your dad was in your apartment."

"My dad?" I interrupt.

He nods. "He's... he's not well at all."

"He's a junkie," I tell him. "Has been for years. I don't ever talk to him. He only calls when he thinks I have money to spare. You saw my apartment," I say with shame. "You know I don't have extra money lying around."

"He was there, strung out. I didn't hurt him, but I was forceful enough that he gave me enough info to let me know you were taken by the SINdicate, and they were in Vegas."

"And how did you get to where Vito is bringing you here to get laid?" I know he can hear the bitterness in my voice.

"Jealous?" he asks sweeping a finger down my cheek.

"No," I answer, which is a lie. I am jealous, and it's a new feeling for me. Men usually don't get this type of reaction out of me. I'm usually the one pushing them away.

"Liar," he says softly and kisses my forehead. "I didn't get into any of this to get laid, Aviana. I told you we needed to wait in Tampa. Why would I jump at some used up women in a fucking brothel?"

His question is serious. There's no bitterness or anger in his tone. "Please answer the question," I say trying not to lose focus on the current situation, but the more he touches me and the softer his voice gets, the harder it is to focus on what we really need to be discussing.

"I went to their casino and pretended to be drunk and down on my luck. Your dad told me they sought him out, that he didn't go to them looking to borrow money. They did the same with me. Took me down an elevator and had me sign a contract and threw twenty grand in my face." He laughs lightly. "I blew that money before I walked out that night. I knew they were watching me. I baited them, hoping for an in. I didn't know exactly how that was going to happen, but they crashed into my motel room after I begged for more time to pay them back, and took me. Their big boss offered me a job as sort of a recovery agent."

I narrow my eyes at him. "I've pretty much become a goon for the SINdicate. I go out and take money off of guys who owe them. The whole organization is pretty fucked up. Loads more going on than I initially realized."

"What do we do now?" I whisper.

"I hate to even ask this of you," he shakes his head. "First, tell me what it's like here. You seem healthy. Are they hurting you? Making you do things…"

I place my hand over his mouth and shake my head no. "I have ten days before the extension they gave my dad is up. The guys that come in look at me and ask if I want to do things with them, but they leave me alone when I tell them no.

He nods but swallows roughly.

I continue, "Vito has offered me a contract to stay here and work off my dad's debt."

He stands from where he was sitting on the bed. "Over my dead, goddamned body," he roars.

Chapter 20
BT

"You didn't let me finish," she stammers.

I can't help the clinching of my fists at my sides. If they think she's going to stay here and be forced to fuck guys to pay off her dad's fuck-up, I couldn't care less about the other women. She's my number one concern at the moment.

"I told him I'd never do that," she finishes.

"But you just walked in here with me. They're going to think you're free game from now on. Aviana, I can't walk out of here knowing they're going to hurt you like that."

She shakes her head back and forth. "That's not how it works. The women here are under contract to service," she crinkles her nose, "the men. If they don't want to, the men choose another woman. I've never seen one of the girls say no and get forcefully taken anyways."

Her information calms my frazzled nerves to a degree but not completely. I stop the pacing across the room I didn't even realize I was doing and sit beside her on the bed again.

"What do you suggest I do?"

"Leave me here and figure out where they are taking the other women." Deadpan. Matter of fact. Leaving no room for question. I shake my head *no* almost violently.

"I can't do that," I tell her. "When I leave this evening, you're coming with me."

"We have to save the other girls, BT." I squeeze my eyes shut. As much as I hate the idea, I know she's right. We can't just scoop her up and take off. The SINdicate would just track her down again. The only way either one of us can be safe is to take down the whole organization.

I have no fucking clue how to do that, but by the look in her eye, she won't take anything less than our best effort.

"You are so fucking resilient. I'm in awe of you," I say softly placing my hand on her cheek and kissing her forehead again.

The woman before me is willing to stay in this place, relinquishing her freedom for as long as it takes to rescue other women she doesn't even know.

She reaches up and places her small hand over mine and another against my chest.

"Aviana," I whisper and tug her face to mine as she looks into my eyes. They flutter closed just before my lips meet hers.

Kissing the woman I never thought I'd lay eyes on again is the most surreal moment of my life. This moment, not swearing into the Army at MEPS, not boarding the plane at eighteen to head to basic, not lying in the sand after the explosion not knowing whether I would live or die. This moment.

The fight against her safety versus the chance to rescue others rages in my head, competing with the blissful feeling of her mouth on mine. I do my best to drown out the part of my brain that's telling me to grab her and run. Realistically, I know I have to destroy this organization before she'll ever be completely safe, but walking out of here and leaving her behind will be the hardest thing I'll ever have to do, and that's saying a lot because I've had to make some really fucking hard decisions after the explosion in the desert.

The sweep of her warm tongue over mine coaxes me to let the other problems rumble quietly in my head and put the majority of my focus on her. I release her face and wrap my arms around her waist. Tugging her closer to me, I never pull my lips from hers. She reaches up and fists my hair in both of her hands, the sensation on my scalp arrows desire straight to my cock fighting the zipper on my jeans.

I pull my mouth from hers a fraction and rest my forehead on hers, our panting breaths mingling.

"I miss your beard," she says softly running her hand over my shaved face.

"Me too," I tell her not opening my eyes. "It'll grow back," I promise.

She tilts her mouth closer to mine, and I can feel the brush of her kiss swollen lips on mine.

"I need to make you come," I say from out of nowhere. "They think I'm in here having sex with you. They'll suspect something if you don't look satisfied." I can't help but feel like an asshole for the words I've just spoken. I can't think of a better way to get my mouth on her while my brain is fried with passion.

"That so?" She pulls her head back from mine and looks in my eyes. I can tell by the look on her face that she's amused by my reasoning. I can also tell she knows I'm full of shit. She leans in closer but tilts my head to the side. She licks and nips my jaw, making her way closer to my ear. "And just how did you intend to act out your plan?"

I groan as she takes my earlobe between her lips and sucks, her teeth gently scoring the flesh erotically.

"Do you want me to explain or do you learn better with a hands-on experience?" I ask softly.

"I retain more information with hands-on experience," she says breathily, moaning in my ear when I cup her ass and pull her against my chest.

The action has her straddling me on the bed. I know this is a crazy situation. She's been kidnapped; I'm being forced to work as an enforcer for the SINdicate, and yet all I can think about is laying her back and putting my mouth on every single inch of her flesh she'll allow. If the grinding of her hips on my erection tells me anything, she wants it just as bad as I do.

"Are you sure?" I need to make for certain this is something she wants and not something she feels forced or coerced into doing.

She nods her head and kisses me fiercely. I stretch out a hand and lower her to the bed, my body staying against hers. The last thing I want is to lose this connection with her. It will end all too soon as it is.

I sweep hair off of her cheek and look down into her beautiful face. She's stunning even as a captive with no makeup. Her hazel eyes are bluer than green in this light, and even though I could get lost in her eyes all night, my body tells me to focus on other things.

How I'm going to leave her once I've had a taste of her, I'll never know. I kiss down her neck and cup her breast in my palm. Her light moans and soft whispers nearly make me come undone. I slide her tank top up her milky white skin, never taking my eyes away as I expose inch by inch of her flesh. The fact that she's not wearing a bra becomes evident when her pert dusty-rose colored nipples are uncovered.

Hunger grows deep in my gut as I lean in with as much control as I can muster and wrap my lips around one hardened nub. I breathe deep through my nose as she arches her back, pressing her perfect breast further into my face. Her fingers dig into my back, and her legs wrap around my waist. I could come in my jeans right now if I thought about it long enough.

Releasing my shoulder from her curled fingers, she tugs my t-shirt up and grips my bare flesh. Not wanting to miss the feel of her skin against mine, I reach down and pull my t-shirt completely off and toss it to the floor. I settle my body back over hers, stomach to stomach and kiss her mouth again.

"I never should've let you leave that night," I say against her mouth.

"This would've still happened. They were waiting for me." I want to hold her in my arms forever, but we don't have time for forever right now. My cock twitches in my pants, reminding me of what else I can be doing.

A gasp, as I grind my hips against hers, is her only answer. Her hands trail lower down my back until they're clutching my ass inside my jeans. How there's room for her hands when my cock is taking up so much room in the front, I have no idea. Her nails dig into my skin as she pulls me harder against her.

"Fuck," I groan and move my hips back a few inches. She sighs her displeasure at the loss of contact but smiles when my mouth lowers to her breast once again. I nip her flesh and make my way to the band of her sweats. I lick across her stomach just under the band of clothing, which is the only thing separating me from my ultimate destination.

I watch as chill bumps spread across her skin from the rush of my hot breath. Sliding further down the bed, I grip the sides of her lounge pants in my hands. I look into her eyes one more time, getting permission to take this next step. She nods slightly and lifts her hips a few inches off the mattress, making it easier to tug the fabric free of her body.

The mouthwatering scent of her arousal invades my brain, shutting down the outside world. The only thing I can focus on right now is getting my mouth on this glorious flesh.

"Jesus," I curse seeing her glistening pink flesh for the first time. I use my thumbs to spread open the sexiest pussy I've ever had the pleasure of laying eyes on.

"BT," she groans and swivels her hips in a delicious circle. I should correct her, remind her she has to call me Mike, but in this second it doesn't even matter.

I go for the gusto immediately. I know we don't have much time, and the last thing I need is to get interrupted. I vow to take my time the next chance I get. Her hips buck up, almost knocking me off the bed. I grin up at her. She doesn't smile back; I don't know if she's even capable of cognizant thought right now. Her eyelids are heavy, her breaths rush out in harsh pants, and she's biting her lip so hard I'm sure she'll draw blood any second.

Wrapping my mouth and lips over her entire center, I suck vigorously. My tongue grazes her swollen clit with soft flutters at first. My own lust and need to feel her convulse against my mouth has me increasing the pressure my mouth has on her.

"Oh God," she moans, gripping a handful of my hair. I cut my eyes from the apex of her thighs to her face. I think watching a woman come undone is one of the sexiest, most erotic things a man can ever be involved in. This isn't about me; it's only about her, but I'd be a liar if I said I wasn't getting pleasure from pleasing her.

I begin to suck her clit in earnest. I pulse my tongue against her in rhythm to the grinding of her hips.

"Fuck," she whimpers. "This is even better than the dream." I smile against her body at the knowledge. I'm not even certain she realizes what she just admitted out loud.

Chapter 21
Aviana

His mouth on me is not quite what I remember from my dream. He's more aggressive than I imagined, but I also miss the scruff of his beard along my flesh. He more than makes up for it when his hand slowly climbs my inner thigh. I'm so wet he enters me easily with two thick fingers. The pleasure he's giving me is out of this world. I want it to last forever, even though I know it will end soon.

For the first time in my life, I'm wishing this man would stay with me. I wish he could hold me all night and allow me to wake up in his arms tomorrow. The problem with those thoughts are that I don't know how much of those feelings are for him specifically or the level of safety I've felt since he showed up. I can't trust anything I feel right now because this situation skews every perception.

BT pulls me from my thoughts the second he curves his two inserted fingers. The tips of his digits stroke that hidden bundle of nerves deep inside of me, causing my back to arch off the bed. My eyelids squeeze tight at the first sharp tingle of orgasm. He moans against my flesh, and the sounds combined with the vibration against my already sensitive clit send me over the edge.

He holds me down with one hand while his other stays buried inside of me. He flicks his tongue rapidly against me, drawing out every possible second of my climax. If I could form thought right now, I'd admit that this is, hands down, the most magnificent orgasm I've ever had in my life.

I lie completely pliable as he tugs my sweats back up my legs, kissing my trembling muscles as he goes.

"What are you doing?" I'm finally able to ask as he pulls my sweats completely up and kisses my stomach.

"What do you mean?" he asks as he dips his tongue into my bellybutton.

I moan again and feel him smile against my skin. "I want you inside of me," I say and begin to shove my pants down my ass.

His hands stop me from going any further than the first curve of my ass.

"We don't have time for that," he says softly settling back over my body.

His weight and the feel of his skin against mine is heaven. I sway my upper body slightly against his, enjoying the feel of his chest hair against the tips of my breasts. He's on his elbows near my face. "I'm going to need more than a handful of minutes once I get the privilege of getting inside of you, Aviana." He leans in and kisses my lips briefly, pulling away too soon. "And it sure as fuck isn't going to be here."

My face falls and the joy I was feeling just a moment ago begins to dissipate. I want to tell him that getting out of here alive isn't a sure thing, and we should take advantage of the time we have. I don't though; rather I look up into chocolate colored eyes that have been keeping me sane in my dreams since the second I woke up in this place.

BT lays to my side and pulls me against his chest. I think the temptation of being lined up against my center was too much for him. I trace the muscles of his stomach as his hand traces the curve of my spine.

"Tell me about this place," he says interrupting the delusion I started to build in my head. For a second, I was pretending that we were away on vacation rather than both of us being under the thumb of the SINdicate.

"The only cameras are the ones at the front door. I've looked, and Darby has confirmed there are no cameras in the rooms. A special key card is required to get out," I tell him.

"Yeah, Vito has to use one to get in as well," he adds.

"I can't believe you're real," I admit against his chest. He kisses the top of my head. "You just came to get me?"

"Yep."

"Just like that?" I tilt my head to look in his eyes.

He shrugs slightly. "Think long, think wrong."

I laugh. "Isn't that a quote from The Patriot, with Mel Gibson?"

He grins from ear to ear. I may not be interested in relationships, but I can openly admit that I'm completely in love with his smile. It lights up his whole face and eyes, and without the beard, the deep dimples on either side of his face are on full display.

"What can I say? I love movies."

I chuckle lightly. "Any other movie bits of inspiration that seem fitting for the night?"

"I have a favorite James Dean quote," he says.

I raise my head again.

"The porn star? Doesn't he usually just grunt?" My eyes are wide, but the crazy thing is, his eyes are wider.

"You watch porn?" He smirks mischievously.

Slightly embarrassed, I lower my head back to his chest. "I'm single and have a healthy sexual appetite."

"I can't wait to get you out of here so I can learn more about this healthy appetite you have, but I'm referring to the actor."

"What's the quote?" I ask. I'm not very familiar with James Dean, the actor, but I know he was a sexy heartthrob back in the day.

"Dream as if you'll live forever. Live as if you'll die today." He quotes.

It's a very profound sentiment. I stay quiet as long as I can, but I feel the need to break the seriousness of how we're both feeling. We both know he'll have to leave soon. I'll have to watch him walk away, and he'll have to walk out of here as if I'm just some girl he met and slept with tonight.

"According to your quote, we should definitely have sex right now." His laughter rumbles in his chest, the sound low and deep against my ear. I smile as he holds me tighter against his chest.

"They have me here in the same building. I just want you to know that so you won't feel so alone," he explains.

I should tell him that I'm still completely alone, and no matter if a few floors are between us, it may as well be a million miles if we can't get to one another.

"I'll come back to you as often as I can. How often do Vito and Frankie come here?"

"I've seen Vito twice I think, and Frankie has been here three times since I got here. Maybe you can persuade them to come more often." I hold him tighter because I know soon he'll be pulled from my arms.

"I don't have much pull with these guys. I'm a means-to-an-end as well. If I hadn't kicked a couple of their asses, I wouldn't even be here."

I don't question him. I have no idea how beating up guys in the SINdicate leads to working for them to pay off debts rather than ending up dead in an alley, but I've never really understood men anyways. I blame that shit on my father. I never could understand why a man who seemed to have everything in life throw it all away to place a bet with his paycheck rather than pay his bills and take care of his family.

I stiffen when I hear Vito's voice near my door. BT hears it too and jumps off the bed.

"I'm so sorry for this, Aviana," he says coming around to my side of the bed. "Sit up," he says harshly and pulls out his semi-erect cock. "I don't want them to want to touch you," he explains quickly.

The locking mechanism makes a whirling sound just as I lower my eyes to his dick. Not caring who's coming in the door, I crane my neck and let my tongue sweep over the head. His eyes go wide, and he hisses a breath between his teeth.

"Time to go," I hear Vito say from behind him.

"Fuck, okay," BT says. "Give me a damn minute."

I watch as he tucks his growing cock back into his pants. I see a pained expression sweep over his face before he turns away from me and walks toward Vito.

"You've got a dud, man," BT says slapping him on the back. "She can't suck dick for shit."

My heart clenches at his words, and a tear rolls down my cheek when he walks out closing the door behind him without saying another word.

I know he's acting. I could see him double in size just being in front of my face. Him warning me about the men and how he wants to make sure no one else tries to sleep with me doesn't make his words hurt any less.

Chapter 22
BT

I hate saying bad things about her, and I hate how I decided to do what I did. I couldn't think of another way around it. The angle of the door to the bed left no other recourse. If I didn't whip my dick out, Vito would've been suspicious. I thought I had more time. It felt like I only had seconds with her, even though I know it was probably closer to two hours.

What I hate the most though is having to walk away from her. I nearly came when I saw her perfectly pink tongue snake out toward my cock. I had to suddenly pull away. If I didn't, I'd never be able to leave her. I may lie to these fuckers about how her oral skills, of which I've yet to experience, sucked, but the tingle in my balls just being a few inches from her mouth tells me whenever I do get to slide to the back of her throat, it will be the best damn day of my life.

Vito notices me holding my hand against my mouth. I can smell her on my face and my hands. I'm pissed I can't just be left in this moment alone so I can enjoy the memory of her on my skin.

"What's up?" He asks indicating my hand.

I sweep it over my chin roughly. "I got pussy on my face," I lie.

He shakes his head in disbelief. "You don't have to do that man. They do whatever the fuck you want."

I shrug my shoulder. "I'm equal opportunity I guess. Waste of my damn time, eating pussy more than half the time. Then the blowjob was less than good." I hate the words spewing out of my mouth, but I need this asshole to think she's not worth his time. I need him to stick with the other girls he clearly feels will do his dick justice.

"You should've just fucked her and got it over with," He says on the ride down to my floor.

"Didn't have a rubber, and she said she didn't know if she was clean or not." I wipe my hand over my face. "Of course she says that shit after she comes all over my face. The last thing I need in the middle of working off my debt is for my dick to fall off too."

He laughs loudly. "There's a bowl of condoms right inside the door." He shakes his head and slaps me on the back as we exit the elevator and make our way to my door. "Next time grab a rubber and fuck her. Maybe she's better on her back than she is on her knees."

I walk through the door and close it behind me without another word. I'm seething. Five more seconds with that guy and the other women would just have to wait for some other guy to rescue them because I'll beat his ass and go get my girl.

We don't have much longer before the timeframe the SINdicate gave her father ends. They know just as much as I do that he'll never come up with the money. I know they may not hurt her so long as they think she's earning some of that money back, but she won't be able to hide the fact that she's turning down everyone but me for long.

Being in this room, only a handful of floors below her makes me crazy. I pace around my small room livid that there's nothing I can do this very second to help her. I regretted leaving her behind the second the steel door closed behind us.

I clench my fists. Every half-cocked plan to rescue her and the other women is no plan at all. Without knowing where the other women are, I have no recourse to even formulate a way to save them and her. I know the first thing I need to do is get a phone off of one of the fuckers Vito and Frankie have me roll.

I've got to get Shadow and the entire Cerberus team on this. Thinking I could handle this on my own and assuming this would be quick and easy was a mistake of epic proportions.

I sit down on the tiny sofa and kick off my shoes. I get up and walk closer to the bathroom. Sitting on the toilet, I remove my prosthetic and the padded socks. Climbing over the lip of the tub is a pain in my ass, which makes me hate the SINdicate more. The only good thing I've discovered with this room is the rate at which the water heats up and extreme pressure the shower head works at.

I lean my head against the wall and allow the stream to hammer my back. I didn't take into account the way my body would feel after leaving Aviana. My balls ache, and the mere thought of her has me thickening without provocation.

I imagine I'm a pitiful sight. At nearly thirty damn years old, I'm stroking my cock in the shower like a fifteen-year-old boy. I can't remember the last time I pictured a specific woman to fantasize about while jacking off in the shower.

I know that coming in the shower isn't going to relieve much pressure. The only thing that would satisfy me right now would be an orgasm resulting from Aviana's direct touch. Her hand. Her mouth. That glorious pussy I had my mouth on a mere few hours ago.

I do know, however, attempting to go to bed without doing something will lead to an already restless night of sleep. I groan as my hand strokes over the engorged head. I lick my lips hoping to get another taste of her. Nothing remains. We kissed so much after she exploded there's not a trace of her on my lips. Fuck. Kissing that perfect mouth, knowing her taste mingled between us, has to be the hottest thing ever.

I stroke myself faster, harder. I picture myself in front of her mouth. I see her trace her tongue over her lips in anticipation. I close my eyes and see her looking up at me, her hazel eyes wide and begging.

"Fuck," I groan as I coat the wall of the shower with long, hot streams of semen.

I take calming breaths, trying to get my heart rate back to normal. I let my mind wander to what life will be like once we get back to Tampa, and we can put all of this shit behind us.

I feel like I can talk to Aviana, even though we've not really had time to talk about anything substantial. I don't have expectations of a relationship with her, even though I hope there will be one. I'm not here to bring her home on the condition that she stay with me, but I can't help but hope she'll want to once we get back.

She will not return to that shitty apartment. She may not live in the worst area of Tampa, but it's in the top five. I'd never be able to sleep at night knowing she's there. We didn't have time to talk about why she left so quickly the night she came to my house for dinner, but I plan to ask her once we get the chance to talk again.

I wash my body and try to think of a way to convince Vito to return to the top floor. I hold absolutely no pull where our daily plans are concerned, but the idea of pussy is very tempting for any man. I know I can't wait to get back up there and get my mouth on her again.

I feel a twinge of remorse thinking about what we did this evening. She's trapped, and even though I may be the only person she can trust right now, I can't help but feel like I took advantage. I'm unexplainably drawn to her, and I know she was begging for more, but that doesn't mean she didn't regret it the second I walked away. That's why I know I can't make love to her until she's free of that place, and the decision is based solely on her wanting me, rather than feeling obligated because of the situation she's in.

Never in my life did I think I'd be dating, or trying to date, a woman held captive by a Vegas mob boss. This stuff is so far-fetched normal people would think I'm crazy if I ever tried to retell this story.

Chapter 23

Aviana

I didn't leave my room again after BT left. The time he was able to spend with me was amazing, and not just because I'm trapped here. He's managed, in only two short moments together, to crawl inside me. Not in the literal sense, even though his fingers, hands, and mouth were an eye-opening experience.

Walls I spent my whole life building have begun to crumble. Last night I spent hours wondering about him and the possibility of more. Normally, I'd shut down any thoughts of wanting a man in my life for more than a little fun, but somehow, he's different.

It's impossible not to want to get to know him better and see where this leads. He dropped everything in his life to come find me. That right there is enough to make any girl swoon. No matter how hard I tried in the beginning, I've discovered I'm in no shape or form immune to his charm. Charm isn't the only thing he has working in his favor. Aside from his ridiculously good looks, he's practically a hero.

If a man is willing to risk life and limb to rescue a girl he hardly knows, what does that say for his dedication to a woman he's actually in a relationship with? I've admitted to myself that the men I've been avoiding to not end up like my mother are nothing like BT. I know I may have shunned a few good guys in my attempt to avoid heartbreak, but not one man prior is as amazing as BT.

I feel absurd lying in bed, fantasizing about what a life with BT would be like. It isn't until my stomach growls, reminding me that I skipped dinner last night to spend time with him, that I force myself out of my room.

I head to the kitchen and make a Nutella and jelly sandwich; my go-to meal these days. The whole floor is incredibly quiet this morning. I head out with my sandwich to find Darby. She seemed pretty excited that Vito was paying attention to her again. I don't see her in the living room area, so I head to her door and give it a soft knock.

It's not early in the morning, but we don't really keep normal hours up here. I blame that on never getting to leave the floor, which means a lot of us take naps throughout the day. When she doesn't respond after the first knock, I try again.

I wait a long minute, and she finally opens the door. My smile fades immediately when I see her swollen eyes. It's clear she's been crying. I gently push my way into her room and close the door behind me. It's not until she sits on the bed and looks at me directly that I can tell she has purple bruising on her cheek.

"What happened?" I ask gently when I really want to get angry and yell.

I knew the women in the house would do something like this eventually, and hate that I wasn't there to help her. I now know that my days of safety are numbered. It's not only the men I have to worry about hurting me but the women as well.

Darby releases a low chuckle. "Vito happened."

"Vito?" I sit down at the foot of the bed. "He hit you?"

She nods yes. "Apparently, he's still upset about the hook ups after my outing with Frankie."

"Did he…?" I can't even get the question about sexual assault out.

"We had sex. It was rougher than normal," she says shrugging her shoulders. "I like it rough, so I was surprised, but it wasn't until we were talking afterward. He told me not to take dates or have sex with any of the other guys. When I explained my contract, he just laughed at me and then he hit me."

I gasp and cover my mouth with my hands. "What does that mean now?"

"It means I'll only be allowed to be with him." She shakes her head and begins to cry. "I can't just have sex with one person. That's not who I am."

I rub her knee because I don't know what else to say. Normally I would know exactly where she's coming from but after meeting and spending time with BT, it seems my views on sex are changing.

I want to tell her about him, but I know I can't. Not just because he told me to keep it to myself, but I know I can't trust anyone here, even if she's the closest thing to a friend that I have.

"I want out," she says through her sobs. "I'm only half way through my contract."

"Can't you just ignore him? Do what you want?"

She shakes her head vigorously. "He told me that if he found out that I hooked up with another one of the guys he'd send me to The Cat House."

"Fuck," I mutter.

"Yeah," she says, "fuck."

***

Darby and I sat in silence for a long while. I didn't leave her room until she said she was tired and wanted to sleep.

I hate that I can't tell her about BT and his plans to rescue me. I don't know how many of the other girls would want to leave when the time comes. My hopes are they would have no choice because the entire SINdicate would be broken up and no longer a working organization. What happens to them then? Will they just be thrown out into the world?

I know Darby's story and how miserable her life was before Vito found her at the strip club. I imagine most of the other girls' stories are similar. Life has to be pretty rough for the idea of living in a brothel to sound like a good plan.

No one here seems to hate it much, but I know when Darby finally comes out of her room, she'll pretend to be just as happy as she pretended before Vito hit her last night. She can't show weakness. Especially not when all the other women hate her. The other girls could be just as unhappy, but I'll never know that because they despise me for just being friends with her.

I curl up on the couch in the living room. If I go back to my room, I'll never want to leave. My sheets smell like BT, and that makes me miss him tremendously. I know that's where I'll end up shortly, but for now, I need a little distance.

I'm flipping through channels when I feel the presence of another behind me. I look over my shoulder and see a tall, model-thin woman. She's stunningly beautiful, and I can see the appeal the men would have when they visit her. Long, wavy blonde hair is braided over her shoulder, and her natural beauty is obvious since she's not wearing makeup. She has a plate of fruit in one hand and a bottle of water in the other.

I smile up at her and hope for a split second that she's here to be nice. I've seen her before. We're in such tight quarters; it's impossible not to see everyone that's here.

She sneers back at me. *So much for hoping.*

"Looks like you're a whore after all," she says maliciously.

My eyes widen. I wasn't expecting that. All of the other women have just kept their distance. They've been rude, but it's been more ignoring and shunning than blatant aggression. The other women may not talk to Darby and me, but apparently they talk to one another. This woman wasn't anywhere to be seen last night when I took BT to my room. A few of the other girls were. Clearly gossip travels fast around here.

I don't answer her because honestly I can't think of anything fast enough. I turn my head back to the TV, doing my best to ignore her.

She won't give up though. I feel her lean down closer to my head.

"You won't last long," she pants in my ear. "Your pretty little ass can't keep up with the guys. You'll be in The Cat House faster than you can spread your legs for the guys."

I turn to look back at her, resisting the urge to flinch away from her hard stare.

"Funny you should say that," I begin with more bravado than I actually feel. "Vito mentioned that's where you're headed if your ass gets any bigger."

My words are harsh, and have no basis in truth; she's practically perfect. As a woman though, I know almost every woman has things they'd like to change about themselves.

She stands to her full height and sputters as if she's trying to come back at me with a witty retort. She fails, miserably. I watch as she slams down the plate of food on the side table and storms off to her room. *Bitch*. I bet she spends the rest of the day throwing up. Landing in The Cat House is the worst nightmare of everyone here, myself included.

Chapter 24
BT

When I'm stressed back home, I hit the gym. To say I'm stressed right now is an understatement. I do as much as I can in my room, but Vito hasn't been generous enough to let me hit the gym. Not like I've asked. He and Frankie are both pretty thin. I'm certain it has more to do with the coke they snort than natural metabolism.

I miss Scout and my normal routine. I need to hear my dad's voice. He's always kept me grounded, but I know that's not a possibility. If I can be successful at getting Aviana out of Vegas alive, it will all be worth it.

A knock at the door startles me temporarily. I take a quick look at the ancient digital clock on the bedside. Vito normally doesn't show up until later in the evening, but if he's here now it means tonight is going to be super fucking busy.

I open the door. "You ready to go?" Vito asks from the hallway.

"Yeah, man. Give me a minute to grab my shirt." I walk back into the room and grab my shirt and a hoodie. It's warm during the day, but the desert gets cold at night.

Hours and several jobs later we're in yet another shitty hotel room. I yank the guy up, but he struggles, and we tilt to the side. Crashing into the bedside table, his flailing arms knock everything to the floor. His cell phone shines like a beacon in the night. I crowd close to him, holding his dirty shirt tightly in my fist. Reaching down with my free hand I scoop up the phone and slide it into the front pocket of my hoodie.

I pull my fist back and punch the guy in the nose. I regret hitting the man, but I have to make it look good. He's another junkie, and I see Aviana's dad in my head as I hit him. He groans and his head rolls on his shoulders. I release his shirt and pilfer his pockets as he slumps, breathing raggedly on the floor.

"Stupid fucker," I hiss as I pull a few dollars out of his pocket.

I hand the meager collection to Vito. He's talking on his phone and paying no real attention to me. He's getting more relaxed around me. Of course, I've given him no reason to doubt my loyalty, even though it's been forced. I've mentioned once or twice about continuing to work for the SINdicate after my debt is paid. He's not given me an answer one way or the other, but his confidence in me seems to be growing daily.

***

The sun can be seen over the horizon before our night is over. That seems to be the schedule in Vegas; awake at night, sleep during the day. My circadian clock is so fucked it will take weeks before it's back to normal.

I never want to work for these assholes, but the phone in my pocket increases my distaste in the twelve hour day we just finished. As usual, Vito hand delivers me to my door.

"Get some rest," he instructs. "Tomorrow will be another long ass day."

I nod my head. We, well I, worked my ass off today. Not that the money I recover will make any difference in the end, but I haven't been pulling hardly anything off the guys the last couple of days. I pull the phone out of my pocket, and it might as well be a gold bar. This thing is more valuable than a truckload of money at this point in the game.

Vito never comes back once I'm in my room, but I shower and wait to make sure today won't be the first time he returns before pulling the phone out. I dial the eight-hundred number Shadow had me memorize. It's a recording for a mattress company. I leave the phone number as instructed and nothing more.

He never told me how long it would take for them to get back to me, and the hour long wait nearly kills me.

The phone rings and I can tell by looking at the number that it's Shadow. The readout is the same as the number I left the message for.

I don't answer with a normal greeting. "I think my crabs have infested my mattress." It's the "code phrase" Shadow insisted on when he told me about the contact line.

His laughter bellows through the phone, and as much as I want to get pissed it actually brings a smile to my face.

"Stupid fucker," I mutter into the phone.

"How's Sin City," he asks after his laughter dies down.

"Miserable," I answer honestly.

"You ready to admit defeat?" His tone is serious now.

"You have no idea," I admit. Most men would feel shame in this situation, asking for help is never easy, but when it comes to requesting it from your brothers, it's easier than most times in your life. These men trained as I did, and we all know that assisting each other is a lifelong commitment.

"Oh, we have some idea. We've had eyes on you since we came and got Kid."

"He's okay?" I ask with relief.

"Well," he pauses. "He's home." He doesn't offer more so I don't ask. He hit that table pretty fucking hard. The thought that he may be paralyzed rests heavy in my gut.

"I found, Aviana," I inform him. "They're holding her in the hotel connected to The Golden Dragon casino. I'm sure Kid told you that I took a loan from the main guy Vinnie. They have me working for them to pay it back. I'm sequestered in the same hotel, but a few floors down from her."

"We can get you both out tonight," Shadow says. "We were waiting to hear from you before we swept the place."

"This organization is much more than giving loans and kidnapping girls when someone can't pay. Aviana says they have another whore house where they force girls into prostitution."

"Another one? Fuck, do they have her in one?" Shadow's voice gets lower, and I can tell how pissed he is at the idea that these men are forcing women into prostitution. He deals with this shit on a regular basis, but the instinct to protect every woman he can never falters.

"Sort of," I tell him and run my hand over my head. "She says the women who are on the top floor are there by choice. They're working a contract and are there pretty much to fuck the men in the SINdicate who don't have time to hunt for pussy on their own."

"And they're making Aviana do that shit?"

"She still has time left on her dad's extension. She hasn't been forced into anything yet. I could kill that fucker with my own hands for putting her in this situation."

"Yeah about that," Shadow begins. "You won't have the chance."

"What the fuck are you talking about?"

"We did some recon on her apartment, hoping to find more info about her dad and the organization. Her dad was dead on the couch. Looked like he overdosed." I let out a heaving breath.

I have no idea what this will do to her. By her own account she had no relationship with her father, but at the end of the day, he was her dad. The loss of a relative, even after all of the hell they've brought into your life is still difficult. The what-ifs and regret of not doing and saying things can be heavy in the heart of the people left behind.

"We called the police. Reported the smell and left. I honestly couldn't believe no one else had called. It was a pretty rank situation," Shadow says when I don't respond to the news of their discovery.

"I don't know how she's going to take the news, but it won't matter if we can't get her out of here safely." The truth of my words isn't as bitter now that I know Cerberus is involved.

"We cleaned out a bunch of her shit, put it in storage. There's no way she needs to come back to that mess."

"I appreciate that, man." These guys think of everything.

"So this is more than the quick in and out? Now we have to figure out where the other girls are being taken." Shadow grows silent on the other end.

"The entire SINdicate needs to be dismantled. They're preying on weak, drunk and drugged out men. Men who have no hope of paying them back. It's bad business all around, but they don't show any signs of stopping," I tell him. "Aviana doesn't want to leave until she knows the other girls can be rescued."

"Brave girl," Shadow praises.

"Extremely," I agree.

"We have quite a few guys on this. It won't be long before we have the intel on where the other girls are being housed. What else you got?"

"Key cards are required to get into my room, the area where the women are at on the top floor as well."

"Those are easy to bypass." Maybe for you, I think.

"We need a day when both of you will be in the same location. We make every effort on every job to ensure the safety of all those involved, but it's easier for us if we don't have to split the teams too much."

"I'll call you back when I know we'll be together. I can't carry this phone with me and risk getting caught with it."

Shadow gives me a direct line to memorize, so I don't have to go through the bullshit of leaving a message again.

"I'll call you when I have more information," I tell him.

"Keep safe, brother." The line goes dead.

I manage to stash the phone inside of the bedside lamp. They haven't tossed the room for contraband, but these guys are mercurial on a good day, so the chance is always there.

I have no idea when I'll get to see Aviana again, but I know the minute I do is not a second too soon.

Chapter 25

Aviana

It's been five, long miserable days since I saw BT last. Darby has kept to herself more than usual. My heart thumps loudly when the double beep of the door echoes through the room. I watch with baited breath as it swings wide and Vito, along with BT and another guy I don't know, walk in.

I train my face to as much impassivity as I can when all I want to do is jump up from the couch and run into his arms. I see his fist clench, and I know he wants to come to me also.

I see Vito slap him on the back and point to the bowl on the small entryway table. BT nods and grabs a condom from the bowl. Just when I thought my pulse couldn't get any faster, it beats at the speed of sound. I swallow thickly as I see him pocket the prophylactic.

I watch Vito disappear down the hall, bypassing Darby's door and choosing the one right next door.

Other girls are milling around, visibly preening at BT as he walks across the room. *No luck, ladies, this man is mine.*

He approaches me and holds his hand out. "Aviana," his voice is husky. "Want to have a little fun?"

I lay my hand in his and stand. I smirk at the blonde bitch that was so mean to me the other day when we walk by.

"Skank," she mutters under her breath.

I don't let it bother me. With BT here, nothing can phase me.

"What the hell was that about?" BT asks as soon as the door closes behind us.

I pull him toward the bed and straddle his lap before speaking. "It seems some of the girls hate me by association. I've made friends with Darby. Hell, she's the only girl who will speak to me." I nuzzle my nose against his neck and feel his hands grip my ass. "From the way they were all looking out there, they're pissed you've chosen me instead of them."

"Mmm," comes his only response when I nip at his ear.

I hear his stomach rumble and pull my face away from him. "Are you hungry? I can make you a Nutella and jelly sandwich," I offer.

He scrunches his nose up. "I'm not hungry for food, and I don't want to waste our time together eating." He smirks. "Well, eating food anyways. Besides, Nutella is some nasty shit."

I narrow my eyes at him and point at the door. "Get out." A moment of confusion marks his face until he sees me smiling. "If you don't like Nutella we can't be friends. Dealbreaker," I tell him and begin to slide off his lap.

He grips me tighter to his chest. "I'm a peanut butter guy myself." I look at him with disbelief. "Seriously! I can't keep the stuff in my house; I'd eat it all in one sitting."

"I guess you can stay," I say with a big smile.

His face grows serious. "How are you doing here, Aviana?"

The mood in the room shifts immediately. I go to climb off his lap, but his hands hold me in place. "What's happened?" His voice is laced with anger and regret.

"Nothing," I answer softly. The look on his face says he doesn't believe me. "Seriously, BT. Nothing has happened. One of the new guys got handsy with me yesterday, but Frankie shut him down. He didn't try anything after that."

"Frankie was here last night?" I nod. I can see the anger in his eyes. "He wasn't with Vito and me yesterday. I assumed he had the day off or something. What else?"

I frown. This is not how I want to spend my time. "Well, I had words with that girl that called me a skank a couple days ago, but she didn't hurt me or anything. Oh," I say remembering my time with Darby after their last visit. "Vito hit Darby in the face. Her cheek was swollen and bruised. It was hard for me not to tell her it would be over soon, but she says she's ready to get out. She doesn't want to be here anymore."

"Everyone will get out, Aviana. I'm working my best to make that happen as quickly as I can." I give him a weak smile. I know he's doing everything in his power, but I don't know just how much power one man can have. I haven't given up hope, but as each day goes by, the time they gave my father dwindles, my safety fading away with it.

"I know you will," I tell him. I twirl a lock of his hair at the base of his neck, and the atmosphere in the room begins to shift.

His eyes shine up at me, and I think we've been talking enough. I lean in and press my lips against his, running my tongue along the seam.

He gives as much as he gets, groaning when I suck the tip of his talented tongue into my mouth. He pulls away too soon, and I grumble my displeasure. He releases my ass and brings a gentle hand to my cheek. "I thought you'd be mad at me because of what I did before I left last time."

My core clenches at the memory of his thickening cock near my mouth. "My feelings were hurt," I admit. "But I know why you did it."

"Vito made me grab that condom. He's going to think I had sex with you," he says tentatively. "I'm going to let him, Aviana. He can't think anything other than sex is going on between us."

I rotate my hips against him, happy to find him hard and ready. He wants me as much as I want him, and I smile with feminine pride. "You don't have to lie to him," I whisper reaching for the zipper of his jeans.

He places a trembling hand over mine, much like he did the night at his house. "Aviana," he says in a pained voice.

His rejection hurts more now than it did then. I lean forward, leaving my hand on him. I place my cheek on his shoulder and sigh. "I want you to make love to me," I plead. I feel him grow thicker under my hand.

"Not here," he says softly.

"I want this." I pull my head off his shoulder and look him in the eye. "I need this. I need to feel like something in my life is a choice." He reaches up and wipes away a stray tear I didn't know I released as it rolls down my face. He grips the back of my neck softly.

"Avi," he says with sympathy in his voice. He tugs me to his mouth. I melt into his gentle kiss, overcome with emotion at his sincerity.

"Not here, not like this, baby." His lips move against mine as he speaks. "I've got help coming; it won't be much longer."

I don't ask what he has planned. I know if he tells me I'll fixate on it and won't be able to think of anything else while he's away. My time here would be more torturous than it already is.

"Let me take care of you," he says sliding the top of my tank lower, revealing the swell of my breast.

His thumb traces the swollen, tightness of my nipple. I arch my back into his hand, needing to feel him everywhere.

"Please," I beg.

He shifts our weight, so I'm on my back on the bed, and he's hovering over me. Sitting back on his knees I watch as he pulls the condom from his pocket. He tears it open with his teeth; the sight causes chills to run over my body. The anticipation of him changing his mind makes my body tremble.

My heart falls when I see him unroll it and toss it and the empty wrapper to the floor. "Have to make it look right."

I don't have a chance to argue when he settles his body over mine and licks his way over my shoulder. With sure hands, he pulls my tank top off and tosses it behind him. He must know I love the feel of his skin because he discards his shirt as well.

He settles back over me, but his height and my shortness keeps his erection from rubbing where I need to feel it most. I swivel my hips in hopes that he'll oblige, but he doesn't. My legs are splayed wide to accommodate his width as he licks and kneads my breast. The course feel of his hands on my flesh makes me groan loudly.

With quicker speed than the first time he visited, his mouth is lowering down my body, and he's tugging my sweats free.

"I'll never get enough of you," he says as his mouth lowers to my wet flesh.

There's no teasing, no preamble this time. The shock of his quick descent has my back arching off the bed. His mouth leaves me, and the only thing I can feel is the rush of his hot breath against my skin.

I look down and find him staring back up at me. "So, you've dreamed about this?"

I nod my head. "Many times," I admit breathlessly. "Reality is so much better."

He chuckles and attacks my clit vigorously. I grip his hair in both hands, my body taking over my brain. My body moves against his mouth roughly without thought.

I whimper as I feel his hand slide up my thigh. I'm well aware of what those fingers are capable of, and the prospect of them in me again is electric. Unlike last time, he teases me with the tips. I shift my hips again trying to get them to slide deeper, but he holds me still with a large hand across my stomach.

"Easy, baby," he mildly chastises, "make it last."

I mumble my frustrations until he slides deeper, his mouth working my clit and moving sensually over my flesh.

"Fuck!" I yell as my orgasm hits with little to no warning. I pulse against his mouth, and he laps at my oversensitive pussy.

"Mr. Cock," Vito says from the open doorway.

BT moves so he's covering my body from the sight of the door. My body is trembling both from the climax and the realization that we've been interloped upon and didn't even realize it.

"Time to go," Vito slurs. We haven't been in here long, so he's either drunk off his ass or high as a damn kite; my bets are on the latter. Darby mentioned he likes coke as much as he likes fucking.

Light fills the empty doorway as Vito wanders away from the door. Brazenly, BT leans in, kissing me with more passion than I've ever felt in my life. My lips are swollen by the time he pulls away.

"Thank you," he says against my mouth.

"I should be thanking you," I admit.

He shakes his head slightly. "Believe me, baby. The pleasure is all mine. Keep dreaming about me, Aviana. I'll be back soon."

He grabs his shirt from the floor, turns and gives me a wink, and closes it softly behind him.

Chapter 26
BT

Vito was so fucked up when he came to the door of Aviana's room he didn't even have a mind to ask me about getting caught eating her pussy. I know he'd be suspicious if he wasn't high. Clearly he believes the girls are only here to be used and not pleasured. Why they want to stay, I have no idea. I was pissed when I had to leave. I was nowhere near done with tasting her. Fuck, she comes like a champ.

I don't know where he went after he dropped me off, but he could easily kill someone if he got on the road. He's never told me where he lives, but I'm almost certain he stays here in the hotel as well. When we leave, we always get the car out of the underground parking and not from the valet area.

I didn't get much sleep last night, but the knock on the door close to seven doesn't startle me. It's the normal time we usually begin our night. What does surprise me is Vito standing in the door with a huge smile on his face. He seems to recover from a bender faster than most.

"What's that smile about?" I ask and turn to grab my hoodie.

"You'll see," he says dismissively and turns toward the elevator.

It's Wednesday night, and if it's anything like the last couple of nights, the night will drag on. I know the weekends are busier than the days in the middle of the week. I hate the fact that I'm having to work for these bastards, but nights that seem like days kill me. It's almost like basic training all over again, when a twenty-four hour period seems like it's a week long. Having no contact with my family, friends, and Scout makes it even more miserable.

A short ride from the hotel later and Frankie pulls up in front of a strip club of all damn places.

"What the hell?" I say looking out the window at the flashing neon lights for the 'fabric-free entertainment.' The verbiage makes it seem like it might be a classy place, but the borderline vagrants I see going inside tells me it's not. I've been to my fair share of places like this, and the first clue that it may be a shithole is the fact there is no valet; the classier places always provide that service.

This place is off the strip. It hasn't gone unnoticed that Vito and Frankie avoid the strip like the plague, but I'm almost certain that all the locals do the same. The guys I've been forced to pretty much mug have been in the darker recesses of town as well.

"Your birthday is Friday!" Frankie says enthusiastically as he parks in the dark lot beside the establishment.

I almost correct him, but remember that according to my ID Mike Hawke's birthday is in a few days.

"We have work to do Friday, so we figured we'd celebrate a few days early," Vito interjects.

Just what I need, fucking strippers.

"We have too much to do, guys," I say hoping we'd go to work instead of this.

"We get the day off," Frankie says with a brotherly slap on my back. The contact makes me cringe, but I can relish the fact that these guys, at least, like me a little bit. Why else would they go out of their way for a birthday celebration? Then realization hits. They want to see strippers, but they're responsible for me. They should've just left me in the damn hotel room all night.

"Why waste our money here?" I ask. "We could easily go to the top floor of the hotel and handle business there." It seems like a brilliant idea to me.

I hear Vito chuckle. "You addicted to Aviana's pussy or something?"

I do my best to control my anger. He's got no business even mentioning her. If I want to keep attention off myself, I have to play by their rules, no matter how much I despise them. I shrug. "Now that I got a piece of that ass I need more. Plus, I don't have to work for it." I smile, and he doesn't seem to realize in the darkness that it doesn't reach my eyes. "You guys have the perfect setup. She'll eventually be used up. What happens when she's not as fresh as she is now?"

I don't know if pressing him for information is a good thing, but I need more intel, and they've not given me any detail about The Cat House that Aviana mentioned.

"Don't worry about her, Mr. Cock," Frankie says slinging his arm over my shoulder. "She's still got a few good years left in her, I'm sure."

I want nothing more than to throw his arms off of me and snap his neck, but that can't happen so I just fall into step with him and make our way to the front entrance of the club.

The smell of sweat, whiskey, and stale cigarettes assaults my nose as we enter the club. Flashing strobe lights do their best to hide the flaws of the women on the stage. I'm equal opportunity, so I love many body types on a woman. I can appreciate skinny girls as much as

I love big breasts and a thick ass, but what this place has is none of the above.

The lighting is horrible which only benefits the dancers as well as the men paying to see the performances. The woman on the stage met her stripper shelf life at least a decade ago. She's either a heavy drug user or in her forties, and I'm not talking hot, MILF-action forty either, because there's sex appeal in a hot older woman as well. This sad soul is wrinkled in all the wrong places, her skin is clearly dry either from too much time in the tanning bed or long days spent in the direct sunlight. Her hair is a mess and fried beyond repair. She's just… nasty.

These women are nothing like the girls back at the hotel, so I'm flabbergasted as I watch Frankie shimmy his way up to the stage and throw down some money at her feet.

"What do you want to drink?" I hear Vito ask from beside me.

I look back to the stage. To get through this night? "Whiskey," I answer. "Lots of fucking whiskey."

I know getting drunk around these fuckers isn't the smartest thing in the world, but fuck if I'll survive without a high level of inebriation.

I sit in a dark booth that Vito indicates as he goes to the bar and retrieves our drinks, praying he brings the damn bottle. Shifting my weight, I feel myself stick to the seat. I nearly vomit as the taste of bile snakes up my throat.

It's just from a spilled drink, I think over and over in my head. Chances are that I'm sitting in years of uncleaned jizz, but if I think too hard about it, I'll get sick. I already felt like I needed to bathe in hand sanitizer just walking through the front door.

"Fuck I hate this place," Vito says sitting beside me and placing a large tumble of golden liquid in front of me.

"Why are we here then?" It's obvious. If he doesn't want to be here, then we should leave. I'd much rather be beating up poor guys than sitting in this disgusting place, and that's saying something.

He angles his head toward Frankie, who's near the stage getting a lap dance from the stripper that was just on the stage. He clearly has mommy issues.

"Frankie's wife left him this morning. For some fucked up reason he loves this nasty fucking place," Vito says and brings his own drink to his lips.

"Wife?" I mean I know guys cheat, the sin is as old as the sex industry Vegas is so famous for, but he's never indicated once that he had a wife to get home to.

"Yeah. A shame really; she was a real stunner too." He shrugs. *Was?* My blood runs cold as Vito shrugs his shoulders. "She's no longer a problem for him, though. I think he sort of loved her, so he's taking it hard."

Ice runs through my veins because I'm certain he just told me that the wife is now dead for leaving him.

"So what you're saying," I begin to press him for information, but the look in his eyes tells me I better not even ask. I reach down for my glass of whiskey. "This isn't really my birthday party?"

He throws his head back and laughs. He's too busy laughing at my words to see the tremble in my hands as I bring my glass to my face. What kind of group am I working with if they can kill their wife and visit a strip club like it's any other regular day?

I tilt the amber liquid up and pour it down my throat. I make sure not to touch the glass to my lips. The last fucking thing I need is catching Hep C in this damn place. The back of my jeans are already covered in previous customers' donations. The idea has me swallowing the entire contents of the glass.

"Hell yeah," Vito says as I lower my empty tumbler. He reaches beside him, pulling a bottle up and refills my glass.

"These women are nasty," I say as another less than desirable stripper takes the stage.

"Keep drinking," Vito encourages. "Sometimes it helps."

I watch as he drains his second glass. I tilt mine back in kind. There is not enough alcohol in this fucking city to help with this place. I glance over and see Frankie in the corner of the club, almost completely shrouded in darkness. I wish he was entirely out of sight because seeing him getting sucked off from the granny stripper is now burned into my mind forever. I groan and pour another drink, wishing brain bleach was a real thing.

***

"We need to go upstairs," I slur as an equally drunk Vito helps me out of the elevator.

"You're in no condition to go up there," he responds. "You couldn't find the wet spot with a map and flashing neon signs."

"I need her." I need to shut the fuck up, but the liquor coursing through my veins doesn't allow me the ability to keep my mouth shut.

"I need Aviana." I reach down and grab my junk. Even drunk I know it needs to look like she's only a quick fuck.

Vito chuckles as he unlocks my door and shifts me toward the bed. "You can see her on Tuesday," he says tossing me unceremoniously to the bed. "Get some fucking sleep. We have a shit ton to do tomorrow."

Tuesday. I get to see my angel on Tuesday. The weekend can't go by fast enough.

"If her pussy is that good I may need to get a piece of that myself," I hear him mutter before the door slams closed behind him.

"I'll fucking kill you before that ever happens" I think before my eyes drift closed.

Chapter 27
BT

Add no rest when hungover to the long list of disadvantages of being an indentured servant to the SINdicate. Vito shows up at my door right on time with a smile plastered on his face. His chipper fucking mood may get him popped in the mouth before the night is over with.

He laughs when I grumble at him. I know he drank as much as I did last night. He must be immune to the aftermath of drinking a half a bottle of whiskey, but he looks no worse for the wear this morning.

"Do you have some fancy fucking hangover cure I don't know about?" I ask as I grab my hoodie from the end of the bed.

"I was drinking before I could walk," he says patting his stomach. "If you were Italian, you'd understand."

I huff at him. Little does he know, my heritage is closer to his that he knows.

"What's the game plan for tonight?" I ask as we board the elevator, hating to watch it descend rather than rise to the top.

"Same as usual. Tonight, though, you may be in for a surprise."

"If that surprise is another nasty strip joint, I'll pass."

He laughs heartily. "Fuck, even I can't do that shit twice in one week. No, tonight you may get the opportunity to see what happens when someone is no longer able to pay back what they owe."

"I'm not a businessman, but why aren't you guys going after people who actually have the ability to pay back what they borrow in full?"

Vito looks at me seriously. "Tempt me not a desperate man," he says.

Shakespeare? Seriously? He's quoting Romeo and Juliet?

"Desperate men do desperate things. Sometimes we get lucky like we did last week with the bank robber."

I nod, not showing any disbelief. How this fucking organization has stayed afloat, hoping people rob banks or knock over liquor stores in an attempt to get the money they owed is the most ludicrous thing I've ever heard.

"Where's Frankie," I ask as Vito indicates for me to join him in the front of the car.

"Police station," he says. I glance at him, but the look on his face says he won't be providing any more information than those two words.

I hope his ass is charged with whatever happened to his poor wife when she got the courage to leave him.

I nod and look out the window as we make our way to yet another seedy ass neighborhood. If they have no problem killing a spouse, then they surely won't have an issue with disposing of me if I become useless to them.

Vito never said they killed Frankie's wife, and other than what I've done to the guys we encounter, there hasn't been much outward extreme violence. Maybe it's my need to see some good in each person I encounter, but I pray no harm has come to that woman.

We pull up outside of a motel the SINdicate clients seem to frequent. I crack my knuckles, preparing my hands for a possible fight. Not many of them take a stand against us, but there have been a few.

Once again the door isn't locked, and we gain immediate access to the room Vito points at. I guess I should count my lucky stars that the SINdicate doesn't have me in a room as nasty as this one. The Golden Dragon hotel isn't exactly a five-star stay, but it looks like it compared to this place.

Sticky, threadbare carpet and warped, ancient furniture fills the small room. Our contact is passed out on the bed with a needle laying close by. Chances are he won't have a penny on him, but that doesn't mean we get to just walk out without rolling him.

"Hey, fucker," I yell kicking the edge of the mattress to shake him awake.

He grumbles but stays asleep. I clear his pockets, finding nothing. I kick at him again, this time making contact with his body. We never let them stay asleep since each one needs to be threatened and warned about what will happen if they don't come up with the money they owe.

He opens his eyes halfway, and I recognize him as a man we made contact with the first couple of days I was forced to work with Vito.

He smiles looking over my shoulder. "My savior," he rasps and closes his eyes again.

I turn back to see Vito spinning a silencer on the end of a handgun. My eyes widen. I knew he had the weapon, but he's never brandished it or felt the need to pull it out to threaten anyone with it before.

Without a word, he points it at the man on the bed and pulls the trigger. The man doesn't move an inch as his life drains out of him from the wound in his forehead. I stumble back away from him.

I'm no stranger to death. I don't know of any solider that has ever left the pseudo-safeness of a base in the Middle East that hasn't experienced death on some level, either at their own hands or the loss of a fellow brother. Seeing someone killed in the civilian world, without the pretext of war is totally different.

I stare back at Vito, trying to regain my composure. If I had any doubt the level of violence this organization is willing to go to, those thoughts have been cleared up now.

"You'll get used to it," he says nonchalantly as he twists the silencer from the tip of the murder weapon.

"Fat fucking chance," I say as he turns to leave the room.

I use my t-shirt to clean the doorknob on the way out of the room and pull the door closed to what has now become that poor fucker's tomb.

***

The rest of the night, thankfully, goes by without more bloodshed. I've never been more grateful to be enclosed in this room than I am right now.

I sit on the bed for a couple hours trying to get my thoughts lined up. My brain tries to make sense of what happened tonight, but no such luck. Evil and abuse surround the entire SINdicate organization.

You'll get used to it.

Vito's words bounce around in my head. I'm no shrink, but I imagine some pretty messed up stuff had to have happened to the man for him to be so blasé about taking another man's life.

I think back to the kids we encountered overseas. We never knew if the kids were in fact part of the organization and there to kill us. They had been raised around death, destruction, and so much hate for American soldiers that they were sometimes even more volatile than their adult counterparts, like baby rattlesnakes, not knowing the amount of venom needed to disable a threat. They go for the gusto every time. I have a feeling that Vito may be the latter.

I shake my head trying to clear the image of that man's blood pooling around his pillow. I stand and retrieve the phone stashed inside the bedside lamp.

I dial the number Shadow gave me last time we spoke. It's four o'clock in the morning, but I know he'll answer.

Two rings and he answers with a gruff, "Urruela."

"Hey, man," I say sitting back down on the edge of the bed.

"How'd you like that strip club?" He asks with a sick chuckle.

"Nastiest fucking place I've ever seen in my life," I answer honestly. "So you guys in town?"

"The whole team got here Thursday. A couple of us got here beginning of the week," he responds.

"They're more sophisticated than I thought," I tell him. "Vito just put a bullet in some guy's skull at the *Paragon*."

"We found him," he answers. "But they're not all too sophisticated. Doesn't take much to put a bullet in someone's head. These guys aren't operating with rules of engagement you expect from an organization."

"It's like being back in the desert," I mutter to him.

"Pretty much," he agrees.

It's true. Thugs, idiots, and assholes kill people every day with no level of organization or skill.

"You find out anything?"

"They carried a girl out the back of the hotel last night." My body stiffens. "It wasn't Aviana," he says easing my mind. "We know where they're taking those girls now. The next move is up to you."

"I need to be with her when it goes down," I tell him.

"I figured," he says lightheartedly.

"They told me we'd go back up there on Tuesday." I look up at the ceiling hoping she's okay. I pray I'm not too late to save her. There's no telling what she's going through right now. I have to trust that while she still has time left on her father's extension, combined with the fact that they think she's 'working off' some of the debt will keep her from harm.

I hear Shadow pull the phone from his mouth and say something to someone else in the room.

"I think we can work it out for Tuesday."

"I have no idea what time we'll go in."

"We'll keep an eye out. We'll move on it around half an hour after you guys enter," he assures me.

A couple of days and all of this shit will be over. Hopefully, both Aviana and I will still be standing when the dust clears.

Chapter 28
Aviana

A soft knock at my door makes my pulse race. It's been too long since I've seen BT and the days seem to be fading into each other. My skin is growing pale, and I know it's because I haven't seen the sun in weeks. In Tampa, I was in perpetual sunshine even though most of my days were filled with pitiful sadness and self-loathing. At least there the sun was always a guarantee. Now I don't even have that. I can tell a horrendous bout of depression is setting in, and there's nothing to keep it away. The promise of seeing BT again is the only thing keeping a little bit of life in my heart.

I get up and answer the door, hoping BT is here to spend time with me. Darby, not BT, is in my doorway when I pull it open.

"Hey," she says weakly.

I open the door so she can pass by and close us into the room. She's been keeping to herself even more than before, but I've avoided everyone also.

"What's up?" I try to say with a semblance of cheer in my voice.

She huffs loudly and plops down on my bed. I climb on as well and sit with my legs crossed Indian style and wait for her to speak. She seems quite comfortable with the silence, so I wait her out.

Long minutes drag by before she finally speaks.

"Vito was here last night." Her words make my heart drop.

I can't help but imagine that BT was with him and chose someone else to spend time with. I've had in the back of my mind that glitz of the SINdicate and all that they do would pull him down eventually. Seems good men don't exist anymore.

"Was he alone?" I don't even try to hide the sadness in my voice. Melancholy and sorrow seems to be her mood as well. Why not be a glutton for punishment?

"He was alone," she says staring at her twisting hands.

I take a deep, relieved breath. "Did he hit you again?" From the way she's ringing her hands together, I already know they didn't have a functional meeting.

"No, he didn't hit me." She sighs loudly. "He was too busy being balls deep in Courtney to even care about what I was doing."

I don't understand her heartache. I don't understand wanting a guy to come back after he was violent the last time.

"I'm sorry," I lie because it's what she wants to hear. I don't know her well enough to chastise her for her choices.

"He stopped by after he got his fill of her. He wanted to remind me that I was still not allowed to mess with any of the other guys." I watch as a tear runs down her cheek. "I'd rather be the focus of a ten-man gangbang than not be allowed to touch anyone."

I laugh because that's ridiculous, but when I look up, I see the pain and seriousness in her eyes. "Sorry," I apologize. "I guess being a..." I let my voice trail off.

"A nympho?" She says with a smirk.

"Yeah, that. I guess no sex would be hard for someone who identifies as a nympho."

I let the silence take back over.

I feel her weight shift, so I raise my eyes to her.

"You know," she begins. "He said I couldn't touch any of the other guys."

I look at her confused. She winks at me, and I immediately understand her train of thought.

I hold my hands up by my head. "Umm, no. I hate the situation you're in, but that's not gonna happen."

She shrugs her shoulders sadly. "I figured it was a long shot, but doesn't hurt to ask."

I'm just about to respond when a knock, followed by the door opening up interrupts me.

Vito stands in the doorway. I watch as he steps aside and BT walks in. I school my face as best I can when all I want to do is smile from ear to ear.

"Be a good little whore," Vito says looking at me. He slaps BT on the back. If looks could kill Vito would be lying on the floor in a puddle of his own blood. "Take care of my boy here for his birthday."

Vito gives Darby a pointed stare making her climb off the bed and leave the room. Vito leans in close to BT, and I hear him whisper. "Tonight's on the house, Buddy. Fuck it up."

Vito closes the door, and I watch as BT closes his eyes and takes a few deep breaths. I know he's trying his best to tamp down his anger at what Vito said to me. I climb off the bed and cross the room to him. I won't allow the outside world and things beyond our direct control ruin our brief time together.

I cup my hand on his face and slide up against his body.

"I'll kill him," he mutters coldly.

"Shhh," I soothe. "I have just the perfect gift for the birthday boy," I tell him as I reach for the zipper of his pants.

He grabs my hand once again. This shit is getting ridiculous. "It's not my birthday. They think it's Mike's birthday," he explains.

I wiggle my hand until he releases it. "Well, then Mike gets a blowjob for his birthday."

He groans but stops my hands when they reach for him again.

"Why won't you let me touch you?"

He takes a step back. "I don't want you to do anything you normally wouldn't do," he says in a frustrated tone.

I look up at him in disbelief. "Seriously? Do you not remember the night at your house in Tampa?"

I let my gaze drop from his. I remember his rejection all too well. Seems all he wants to do is reject me or put his mouth on me. I'm not complaining about the latter by any means, but I want to please him also.

"You rejected me then too," I say softly.

"You wanted to fuck that night." His voice is gruff and a straight arrow to the truth. "I could see in your eyes you didn't want anything more than that."

"It's different now," I tell him.

"Is it? How do you know? You're a prisoner here. I'm practically their captive as well. How can you make informed decisions right now?"

I shake my head at him. "I'm not some traumatized little girl, BT. I'm a grown woman, making adult choices. If you don't want me to suck your dick, then fine. I won't, but don't turn this back on me. I'm not the one pushing against us."

He closes his eyes briefly. I'm mad, and this is not the way I wanted to spend our limited time together.

"I don't want you to feel used, Aviana. I want you to know that these four walls and your familiar face is not the only reason I'm standing here with you and not in one of the other rooms."

"I know that already, BT. You came all this way to save me. I don't want to be with you because I feel obligated. I want to *be* with you. If I ever get out of here; if we ever get the chance to go back to some normalcy. I want there to be an *us*. I'm not pushing you away like I did when you turned me down in Tampa." I sigh, hoping I'm making sense. "And I'm not pulling you to me because of our current situation either."

He cups my face in his huge hand. "Say it again," he whispers.

"I want there to be an us," I say with a smile.

He leans in and slowly takes my mouth in a passionate, all-consuming kiss. He strokes his tongue over mine as if we have all the time in the world, as if both of our lives aren't complete chaos at the moment. I whimper when he tangles his hand in my loose hair, his grip displaying an urgency his lips don't match.

"Let me," I say pulling my mouth from his.

He doesn't stop me when I reach for his zipper this time. I sink to my knees and pull his jeans and boxer briefs down as I lower. His throbbing erection is mere inches from my face and my mouth waters at the sight. I rub my cheek against it and kiss his lower belly.

"Aviana," he gasps. I frown when he begins to tug his jeans back up. "I'm going to fall if I don't sit down."

He shuffles to the bed and sits down near the edge. I don't even bother to get up; rather I opt to walk on my knees until I'm between his legs again.

Placing my hands on his trembling thighs, I run my tongue up the length of him. His cock jerks pulling further from my mouth. "Control yourself, Mr. Urruela," I chastise.

"Not fucking possible." He hisses loudly when I take the plush head into my mouth and give it a hard suck.

I moan at his enthusiasm and pull him deeper in my throat. Grabbing the base, I hold him upright at the perfect angle for my attention. I close my eyes and breathe him in. Manly. Seductive. All mine.

I feel his long fingers tangle in my hair. At first he rests it there increasing our connection, but the deeper I go and the harder I suck the tighter his grip gets. I love the small bite of pain I feel at the roots when his hand begins to dictate my speed and rhythm. I love that he's able to enjoy it enough to exert his control.

I release him and place both of my hands on his muscular thighs, allowing him to take over. He gags me a couple times but listens to the cues and changes his tempo to correct it.

Breathing through my nose is growing increasingly difficult, much like my ability to keep from touching myself. He's lost in the moment, and I cherish it. I feel him thicken just before he begins to spurt hotly in my mouth. I struggle to swallow the salty thickness as it flows out in a torrent. I release him from my mouth and lick around the base, collecting the stray droplets.

"Fuck, Aviana." His voice is hoarse, and it makes me smile.

I lick my lips one last time and wipe away the remaining wetness with the back of my hand.

He lies back on the bed and covers his face with his arm. His breathing is still erratic, but he reaches for me. I climb on the bed and curl up beside him.

"I can't wait to get you out of here, baby. The things I have planned for you. I hope you don't have anything to do in the immediate future, because I think it will take weeks before I let you out of my bed."

Chapter 29
BT

"You better put that thing away," she says jokingly. "You don't want Vito to catch you with your dick out."

Begrudgingly, I tuck myself back into my jeans, even though I was enjoying the coolness of the air after Aviana's hot, talented mouth.

I pull her tighter against my chest. I want to tell her that it ends tonight, but if something goes wrong, I don't want to have wasted one single second of the bliss I feel when she's in my arms.

"It will be over soon," I assure her without a time frame commitment.

"They know who I am," she says weakly. "They'll just come after me again. It will never be over. I'll never be safe."

I feel the wetness from her tears as they soak into my shirt.

"Things will work out. Once it's all said and done, you'll never have to worry about the SINdicate again," I promise her.

"Besides, we can always move from Tampa. LA would be a perfect place for a beautiful, budding actress like yourself."

She laughs against my chest. "I do not want to be an actress."

"What happened to your life dreams of being a showgirl?" I raise my head up to speak to her, but she keeps her head on my chest. "What do you want to do, Aviana?"

I feel her shake her head gently.

"Don't do that, baby. Don't shut me out. Tell me," I prod gently.

"I've always wanted to go into sports medicine," she admits softly.

"Look at me." I tilt her head up with my finger under her chin. "If that's what you want then that's what we do."

"We?" She asks gently.

I nod. "We."

I can tell by the hitch in her voice when she asks that she wants there to be a *we*. My heart soars, because all of this time I was questioning whether we're growing closer only because she's been trapped here for weeks. All of the uneasiness about what happens when we leave hasn't dissipated, but the worries have settled some.

I feel her head lift slightly off my chest as if she wants to speak to me but then she settles back down. After doing this two more times, I shift my weight where she's on her back, and I'm hovering over her.

I look into her beautiful hazel eyes and let my eyes trail down her cheeks. I twitch in my jeans when my eyes land on her plush, swollen lips. Knowing how they got that way nearly has me begging for more.

Under my gentle scrutiny, she finally speaks. "I didn't know if you were here out of some sense of duty or if you were here because you wanted me." She looks away from me, angling her face toward the bathroom door. "I've been in this room wondering what is going to happen if I ever get out of here." She turns her face back toward me, and I watch as a tear slides down her face, disappearing into her hairline. "I didn't know if you had any plans of keeping me after I left."

I smile down at her and push stray hair off her cheek and behind her ear. "You think I can let you go?" I ask softly. "I let you walk away from me once, and you see where that got us?" I chuckle lightly, hoping the mention of her abduction night doesn't upset her too much.

She cups my face with her small hand, and I lean into the gentle touch. I love it when her hands are on me; almost as much as I love my hands on her.

"You seem to have it bad, Mr. Urruela." The corner of her mouth lifts up in a smirk.

This woman amazes me. Her positive attitude and ability to see the fun and possibility in every situation floors me. Her personality and mine go great together.

"You have no idea," I admit on a growl before leaning in and taking her mouth with mine.

I settle more of my weight on top of her and let my mouth explore hers. I grip her hip in one hand and hold her flush against my body. She's squirming and shifting her hips, trying to find the perfect amount of pressure against her, attempting to entice me into action.

My control this evening is absolute. Were it any other night and we'd gotten as far as we had today it would be another story, but I know what's coming, and there's no way I'm going to experience coitus interruptus with the Cerberus MC guys.

I sigh lightly with my lips against her neck, praying that this time tomorrow we'll both be free of the SINdicate and able to do what ever our hearts, and in this case, our bodies desire. I'm as hard as steel but won't let my body control my actions.

"Stop," I say gruffly against her lips. I clamp my hand down on her hip to keep her from grinding against me.

"Please," she whimpers.

"Soon," I promise her.

"I need you," she says before scraping her teeth down my neck.

"Jesus," I pant loudly. The feeling of her damp heat against my jeans makes my brain go haywire.

I know when I finally get her beneath me completely naked we're going to be explosive. She's writhing under me, desperate for me, and I'm loving every second of it.

I know there's a slim chance that tonight might not turn out the way we both want it to. I know that there's always a chance that something could go wrong, no matter how good the Cerberus team is. Knowing this, I refuse to leave her like this.

If something terrible does happen, I want her final memory of me to be one of sated happiness, not uncontrollable need.

I shift my weight to her side and slowly guide my fingers down her taut stomach. The way her muscles jump at the gentle glide of my fingers brings a smile to my face. I get the feeling that if we make it out of here safely, my face will hurt all the time from the smiles she induces.

She gasps when I sneak my hand past the elastic band of her sweats, my intent becoming clear.

A groan rolls from her throat as I push my fingers down her outer lips, avoiding her clit. My fingers converge below the sensitive bundle and plunge into her. She's hot, tight, and so fucking wet. She clutches at my arm with both her hands and I watch as she parts her lips on a gasp and her eyes flutter closed.

Her body temperature increases, and I instantly hate that I'm clothed. I'm desperate for her, desperate to feel her warmth against my skin. Sliding my thumb up to give her the pressure she needs, I growl into her mouth as her muscles clench trying to pull me deeper.

I circle her clit aggressively as my control begins to waiver. The second her body begins to tremble, convulsing around my fingers, I reach for the zipper of my jeans. My body is in control now, leaving my poor brain in the proverbial dust. I feel the bite of her nails on my arm as she peaks. I could come like a pubescent boy at the sounds she's making.

"Aviana," I gasp tugging her sweats down and widening her legs.

Not even bothering to yank my jeans down any further than required for the imminent task, I shift my body between her thighs. My pulse is pounding in my ears as I line myself up against her drenched core. I take a calming breath, knowing I can't go at her the way my body is demanding that I do.

She reaches for me, her fingers slowly teasing my chest and abdomen. I lean forward and watch her eyes as I push my bare cock slowly inside her.

A tremendous boom sounds outside in the hall, setting every individual nerve in my body on edge.

"Fuck!" I yell shifting my hips back and withdrawing from the only place in this world I want to be.

I shuffle off the bed and shove my disobedient dick back into my jeans. Aviana is staring at the door with wide eyes.

I lick my fingers, because what man in their right mind is going to let her taste go to waste?

"BT?" She asks, the fear clear in her shaky voice.

"Get in the bathroom and stay there until I get back," I tell her as I help her pull her sweats up, regretful of covering the Eden I felt for only the briefest of seconds.

Chapter 30
BT

As I watch her back retreating to the en-suite the door to her room bursts open.

"Urruela!" A masked man yells at me gaining my attention.

I turn to him and catch the weapon he's tossed to me. The Sig feels like home in my hand, but I wonder if it's enough. Looking at the man in front of me dressed in full combat gear, makes me feel naked and exposed. I've never felt less prepared for a mission than I do right now.

"It's go time," the unfamiliar voice tells me as I make my way to the door.

Women screaming and a wall of smoke greet me as I leave the sanctuary of Aviana's room. Mindful of her being in there alone, I pull the door closed behind me. The frame is shattered, and the door can't lock now that it's been damaged. An uneasy chill runs up my spine at leaving her so unprotected.

I follow behind the man who retrieved me and make my way deeper down the hall. I've never been to any of the other rooms the times I've been here. The entryway and Aviana's room are the only places I've been. Hindsight hits me in the gut, knowing I should have done more to canvas my surroundings the times that Vito has brought me here.

We stop in front of the door I know to be Darby's room and presumably where Vito should be. On the other guy's count, I wait impatiently as he kicks the door in.

I step inside the room with my weapon pointing at the back of Vito's head as he snorts a thick line of coke off of Darby's tits. She's tied to the bed, tears rushing down her cheeks. I see red whelps all over her body. I'm not really into the BDSM scene, and to each their own, but I can tell by the terrified look in her eyes, that this isn't something she's agreed to voluntarily. I see red.

Vito looks up with a stupid grin on his face, clearly so coked out of his mind that he didn't hear Armageddon happening on the other side of the door.

"Get up fucker!" I yell at him.

He slowly rolls off of Darby, and I see the flash of silver, hearing the sound of the gun before my body can react to his intentions. I feel my body shift slightly and wait for the pain that as a civilian I never thought I'd experience again.

I look down and see the bullet hole in the jeans of my right leg. I smirk at the stupid asshole. His eyes go wide as if he's seeing a miracle occur right in front of his face.

Feeling invincible I stalk toward him, knocking the gun from his hand. Thankfully he's so fucked up that his reaction time is off.

I raise the butt of my weapon and bring it down hard against his jaw.

"That's my favorite leg!" I grunt out slipping my firearm into the waist of my jeans.

I hit him, again and again, providing my own judgment against his face. "For Aviana. For Darby. For all the other women trapped here and abused." I land a strike against his jaw with each sentence.

He's a bloody mess by the time I'm pulled off of him; sure I'd beat him to death if strong arms hadn't pulled me from his chest.

Two other guys come into the room, one tying Vito up, uncaring of his injuries and the other covering Darby with a sheet and loosening her restraints.

"Shit," I mutter wiping sweat and blood from my forehead with the back of my hand.

"Let's get you looked at." I turn toward the voice and watch as a familiar face is uncovered from the black baklava. I recognize him as one of Kincaid's men from the clubhouse. Noticing the look on my face he says, "Snatch," as he reaches his hand out to mine.

He takes another quick look down at my injured leg. "We have a medic outside."

I smile and pull up the leg of my jeans revealing my carbon fiber limb. "Right on," he says with a big grin.

We both make our way out into the hall. I see two other men tied up against the wall, and all of the women huddled together sobbing and crying, unsure of what is going to happen after tonight. If I'm being honest, I have no idea what their futures will look like.

I do, however, have some clue what mine is going to look like. I skirt past Kincaid's team who is also joined by men from several other federal organizations and make my way back to Aviana's room. I smile when I see Shadow standing sentry in front of her door.

Before I can push her door open, a hand clasps on my shoulder. I turn and look into the dark eyes of a man with FBI in bold letters across his chest. I raise my eyebrows at him and glance over at his hand still on my shoulder. He pulls it away with a laugh.

I feel Shadow step in beside me. "Jones," the fed in front of me says extending his hand. I shake it firmly.

"We were wondering how superstar BT Urruela got tangled up with the SINdicate," his gruff voice advises with a smile.

I scoff at him. *Superstar?* What the fuck is that?

I give him a confused look. "We've been watching the organization for some time," he explains. "We would've pulled you out immediately but after looking at your background, we decided against it. We didn't know exactly what you were doing until one of my guys ran into Brighton here down in Tampa." He angles his head to Shadow. "He explained everything to us, and we knew we had an ally in you."

My palms are itching to get back to Aviana, and the thought of her leaving here unnerves me.

"What about the rest of them?" I question as I watch men drag an unconscious Vito and drop him unceremoniously beside his other men.

"I'll explain it to you later," Shadow says in my ear with a clap on my shoulder.

I look into his eyes and understand his intentions immediately.

"I need to get my girl," I say. He nods, knowing my mind isn't on the situation happening out here any longer.

"Damn right you do," he says with affirmation.

Chapter 31
Aviana

Quivering in the bathtub, I let every worst case scenario pass through my head. I squeeze my eyes shut as I hear yelling, and several more small explosions occur outside of my room. The sounds are deafening and more than a little terrifying.

He said he'd come back for me, and I know his best intentions are to do just that. My mind, however, has already pictured him injured or even worse. I grew up in a poor, horrible neighborhood, toughening me up more than most people, but the sounds going on outside this room are unlike anything I've encountered before.

The women screaming are awful, and I can't tell if the people out there are here to help us or hurt us further. I'm a trembling mess when I feel the air change around me. I can tell immediately that the bathroom door has been pulled open.

I do my best to shrink within myself as I feel someone draw nearer to the tub. Suddenly the shower curtain is pulled back, and the end of a long rifle is pointed at me. I screech and look from the gun to the masked man holding me in his sights.

"Aviana Maguire?" He asks with a smooth voice. I nod my head, unsure if he's here to hurt me or not. Relief washes over me when he lowers his weapon, and his posture becomes more relaxed.

"Help me," I say with a tiny voice.

"I can't do that, darlin'," he says.

The tears begin to fall harder, and my whole body starts to shake. I made a mistake; this man isn't here to rescue me, he's here to cause further harm.

"Calm down, sweetheart." He takes a closer step, reaching out his hand toward me. I cower lower in the tub. I keep my eyes on him even though I want to look away and hide from whatever is coming next. "I wouldn't take this moment away from him. Stay here. BT should be here any minute." He pulls the curtain closed again, and I hear his heavy boot steps as he walks away. Closing the door behind him, I'm again shrouded in darkness.

All I can do is sit and wait like I've been instructed. I take the time to wonder if I'll ever not question a stranger's intent when they approach me. I hope I can be able to trust again, but I know that's not something that's going to happen in the near future.

I freeze when the bathroom door opens again. I don't know how long I've been huddled in the dark. It has felt like an eternity even though I'm certain it's only been an hour or so. I know who it is before he can fully get in the room. My body attuned to his; my soul reaching out to its mate.

The shower curtain is pushed back and the next second BT's figure is revealed. My eyes widen when I see the blood on his hands and shirt. He looks down, noticing where my gaze has settled.

"Fuck, sorry," he says and turns to the sink.

"Are you hurt?" I ask watching him scrub his arms clean.

"No, baby. I'm perfect," He answers. He turns back to me and shrugs out of his bloody shirt.

"Whose blood is that," I question pointing to the discarded garment on the floor.

"Don't worry about that, Aviana."

"Are we free?" I'm still crouched down in the tub, terrified that it's not over.

"It's over, baby. Come here." I can see his hands trembling. I can tell he wants to reach out to me, but he's giving me the chance to come to him as a woman, not a captive of the SINdicate.

I scramble out of the tub and into his arms. The tears and sobbing begin again, only this time due to relief and joy rather than heartache and fear.

He whispers calming words and solace in my ears as he holds me tightly against his bare chest.

"It's over," I repeat through my uncontrolled emotions.

"The feds are going to need a statement from you," he says after long minutes of embracing.

"The feds?" I pull my head back to look him in the eye.

I had no idea what was going on outside the room, and the knowledge that federal agents were involved floors me.

Giving in to my confused look he explains. "I'm friends with a motorcycle club from New Mexico. They helped me get to Vegas with Mike Hawke's identity."

"Okay," I say drawing out the last syllable, still not understanding.

"I can't go into detail, but they have a lot of friends in some pretty high places, including federal agencies. They all worked together to take down the SINdicate." He nuzzles my neck as if he can't get close enough to me.

I have a million questions, but none of them matter as long as I'm safe and in the arms of this perfect man.

"Let's go, Avi," he says backing slightly away from me. I feel the loss immediately. "The sooner we give them our statements, the sooner we can get out of Vegas."

I nod my head in agreement and wipe the remainder of my tears off my face. If a statement is the only thing standing in the way of finally being a free woman, then I'm all for it.

***

I didn't have much to give the feds. They knew I was locked up in that building for weeks with no way to escape, which only allowed for very limited interaction with the men of the SINdicate. Honestly, I'd only seen a handful of the men, having only ever really talked to Vito and even that interaction was minimal.

They deemed me lucky since I wasn't injured or sexually assaulted while I was there. They wouldn't give me any information in exchange for what I gave them, but from the way they acted I can almost guarantee that some of the women there and at The Cat House didn't fare as well.

BT and his involvement with the closer working of the organization took much longer to debrief. The hours he was closed in the room speaking with an entire team of men I spent in a quiet room with the other women from the harem.

Thankfully, Darby was there with me, and I didn't have to spend it with the other women. If telling by the sneers I'm getting from across the room, who still hate me. From the look on Courtney's face, they hate me more now than they did before.

"Don't pay her any attention," Darby says pulling my gaze from the huddle of women across the room.

I look at her and sigh. She has the beginning of a black eye, and I saw the marks on her legs and back earlier before we left the hotel. Vito was extremely brutal to her this evening, and I can tell by the look in her eye that she's incredibly thankful for the opportunity to escape.

"We're heading back to the Cerberus Motorcycle club," I tell her, giving her the information BT gave me on the way to this office. "They're in New Mexico." I give her a weak smile. "You could come with us," I offer.

She perks up slightly. "How long will you stay there before returning to Tampa?" she asks timidly.

I shrug my shoulders. "I don't know. Not long I imagine, but you're welcome to return to Tampa with me as well."

"Anything to get out of Vegas," she says.

I nod my head in agreement. Another minute here in the desert is still a minute too long.

We chat for a while longer, my gaze roaming steadily over the door to the hallway that leads to the room BT is in. I know I'm safe. BT assured us we were, but being told to stay here until someone retrieves us is still an uneasy feeling.

I thought leaving the hotel meant clear freedom, but my gut is twisting knowing I've been told not to leave. I twist my fingers in my lap and do my best to keep from shaking my legs as I wait.

I feel Darby scoot closer and wrap me in a hug. "It's going to be okay," she promises.

I should be comforting her. She's been through more hell tonight than I have been in my entire life. It makes me feel like shit that she's forced to comfort me rather than the other way around.

"Fuck me," I hear her whisper the same time a door opening registers in my ear.

I look to her first then at the open door. A tall, muscular man wearing a leather motorcycle vest stands in the doorway. His hair is cut in a close Mohawk, and he's covered in tattoos, more ink than I've ever seen in my life, and that's saying something because I live in Tampa where people seem to wear more ink than clothes most days.

He's looking my direction, but I can tell his focus is elsewhere. I cut my eyes to Darby and see her staring at the man with her mouth slightly open.

I feel him approach as I continue to stare at Darby's reaction to the man.

"Temptress," I hear his husky voice say as he holds out his heavily tattooed hand out to her.

"Darby," she corrects in an equally husky tone as she places her hand in his.

"Snatch," he replies. I watch as his thumb strokes the top of her hand. I glare at him, thinking he's disgusting until I see the black and white patch on his left chest that says the same word, more than likely his road name.

"I'm sure," Darby replies, and even as an outsider I can hear the innuendo.

Without pulling her hand from his, she looks back at me. "I think New Mexico is a perfect place to go," she says.

Chapter 32
BT

I hold Aviana tightly against my chest as she sleeps. I'm thankful the MC has let us tag along with them back to New Mexico, and I'm even more grateful for the private jet we're in rather than facing an eight-hour drive back to their clubhouse.

I smile when I look across the small aircraft and see Aviana's friend Darby none the worse for wear as she tips back a martini, never taking her eyes off of Snatch, the biker that assisted with the entry into her room. This woman has sensuality coming off of her in waves. It doesn't bother me. With Avi in my arms, I seem to be immune to her seductiveness. Snatch, on the other hand, isn't so lucky. He's not speaking to her, but I've seen him adjust his cock in his pants no less than half a dozen times.

I kiss the top of Avi's head and feel her shift slightly in my arms. Looking down I see her peering back at me. I sweep a lock of her blonde hair from her face and trail my fingers down her chin and smooth neck.

"Hey, baby." I kiss her head again.

She blinks up at me, and I can tell by the look in her amazing hazel eyes that I'm exactly what she wants. My chest feels tighter, and my pulse speeds up.

I've fallen in love with this beautiful woman. My entire being is full of a love so strong no other person in my life has even come close to gaining.

"I love you," I whisper to her, unwilling to let a second go by without her knowing it. Never again will I leave things unspoken with her. Begging her to stay was on the tip of my tongue the night she was abducted, and fuck if I don't regret not saying those words.

I watch a small smile spread across her gorgeous face and a tear rolls out of the corner of her eye. She releases a small, content sigh and snuggles deeper into my embrace. She doesn't say it back, which honestly is disheartening, but she didn't jump out of my arms, and for a woman who doesn't do relationships, that's a plus.

***

Our arrival at the clubhouse is chaotic and full of more fanfare than I could've ever imagined. Some of the guys on the team had been gone as long as I was and clearly, they were missed by the others.

Beer is flowing, bikers are together in small groups, and I've never seen so many exposed tits outside of a strip joint in all my life.

Topless seems to be the theme of the night, even most of the bikers are without shirts, although they all wear their leather cuts.

"Wow," Aviana mutters sticking closer to my side as she takes in the scene in front of us.

"It's not usually like this," Shadow says handing me a beer.

I feel Aviana lift her head from my shoulder and turn her gaze to him almost in recognition. I watch as he winks at her and walks away.

"What was that about?" I ask her, setting the domestic brew on a nearby table.

"Nothing," she says with a timid smile.

Before I can grill her further, I see Kincaid walking toward us.

"Aviana this is Kincaid. He's the club president." I watch as they shake hands and exchange pleasantries.

"I kept a room available for you guys," he says holding out a key on a small keychain. "Figured you'd be super tired after your ordeal and would want to turn in early." He winks at us and walks away. What the hell is up with all the winking?

"You tired?" I ask looking down at the beautiful woman in my arms.

She smiles and nods her head enthusiastically. "Exhausted."

The gleam in her eyes tells me we won't be getting much sleep tonight.

The keyring Kincaid has handed me has a very distinct, familiar emblem on it. This belongs to the same room I had before all of the shit went down in Vegas. I escort Aviana down the narrow hallway to the room and lock the door behind us.

She turns in my arms and kisses my clothed chest. I tilt her head back and kiss her chin.

"If you're tired?" I begin.

She shakes her head back and forth, "I slept most of the way here."

My hands are trembling. This is the first time since I've met her that I've walked into a room knowing how things will go. It's the first time, other than the first night at my house, that we've been alone with a slim chance of getting interrupted. We've waited so long for our time together; fought tooth and nail to come out on top. I've been less than patient, but now I have a desire to take my time and love her like she deserves.

I'm a grown man, an Army veteran. I've been chewed up in war and spit out mangled. I'm a survivor. I overcome. Yet, the sight of this woman in my arms holds me captive. My nerves are not about sex or worry over performance issues. My heart thunders in my chest because I know that tonight is the beginning of my future with Aviana Maguire.

    She places her hands on my chest, one directly over my pounding heart and the other slides down and rests on my hip. Without a word spoken, I drag my hands down her sides and grasp the hem of her shirt. Torturously slow, I pull it up and over her head. Her hands fall back into position on my body.

    Her immaculate breasts are front and center, slightly pushed together from her raised arms. I raise my hands and run my thumbs over hardening nipples. Her head lolls slightly on her shoulders, and I feel the hand on my hip slide from its position. Small fingers dip into the waistband of my jeans, teasing the sensitive flesh of my lower stomach.

    I gasp when her soft fingertips brush the tip of my cock which is straining against the zipper of my jeans begging to be released. I pinch her nipples and roll them between my thumb and forefinger, causing her to tug my jeans and pull me flush against her body.

    Releasing her breasts, I reach for the hem of my t-shirt and begin to pull it off. Her hands land on mine and I see her shaking her head slightly.

    "Please, let me," she whispers taking over.

    I lower my hands to my sides and let my eyes close. The feel of her hands on my skin as she slowly raises my shirt up is a heaven I've never felt before. This woman owns me and I never even spent a full night with her.

    "Bend down," she says softly.

    I open my eyes to look down at her and realize I'm too tall for her to pull my shirt off completely. I raise my arms over my head and bend at the waist. The action puts my head close enough that I can feel the heat rolling off of her body, more importantly, her amazing breasts. Not one to waste an opportunity, I swipe at one of her nipples with my tongue.

    In reaction, she stands taller on the tips of her toes and pushes further against my mouth. Lowering a hand, I palm her neglected breast while I continue to feast at the delicate skin of her left one. Dexterous fingers tangle in my head, my t-shirt completely forgotten.

    "Jesus, baby," I moan when I feel her hand grip me through my jeans.

I kiss up her chest, over her shoulder, and along her jawline. My mind wants slow, sensual lovemaking, but my body is insisting on throwing her on the bed and going at her like a maniac. The internal war is raging, but my body remains still as she unsnaps the button on my jeans and lowers the zipper.

Leaving my jeans on and around my waist, her hands delve under the waistband of my boxers, one seeking my throbbing cock and the other cupping my balls. I grind my teeth unconsciously at the sensation of her cool hands on my heated flesh.

Just like she did back at the hotel, she edges my jeans and boxers down my legs and hits her knees in front of me. Fuck she's beautiful, all hazel eyes and honey blonde hair looking up at me. The sight of my cock protruding so dangerously close to her mouth has it twitching in anticipation.

She slips my shoes off and removes my jeans, tossing them carelessly to the side. Her delicate, tender hands stroke all the way up both legs, paying each one equal attention as she stares up at me. She doesn't waiver in her ministrations when her fingers hit my prosthetic for the very first time, and I've never felt more whole in my entire life than I do at this moment.

Her lips glisten as she runs her tongue over them. I see her eyes dart to my cock quickly as if she's judging distance, but then they return to mine. Feeling overheated, I rip my shirt off and let it flutter to the floor to join my other clothes. Leaning in a few inches to close the distance, her tongue reaches out and with the softest of touches, she licks away the beaded drop from the tip.

My lips part and my eyelids lower. I resist the urge to grab her head and jut my hips forward. The tips of my fingers tingle with the need to touch her. Resting both of her hands on my thighs, she slides her insanely hot mouth over the head and halfway down my shaft. I could stay here forever, nestled in her mouth with the tantalizing feel of her tongue circling my rigid cock.

She releases a slight moan, and the sensation reverberates through me, landing in an echo deep in my gut. I don't know if I'm going to be able to control myself enough to go slow when I get inside of her, but coming down her throat is not in the cards tonight.

"Come here," I say reaching down and motioning her to stand. "Fuck," I mutter as she takes me to the back of her throat one last time before standing.

Mirroring her actions, I tug her sweats down and crouch on the floor. Freeing her feet of shoes and then removing the tangle of her pants, I throw her left leg over my shoulder and lean in close to the apex of her thighs. I run my nose at the juncture of her leg where it meets the rest of her body, relishing the feel of her hands tugging my hair.

She smells amazing. Womanly. Ready.

Her glistening flesh urges me forward and without preamble, I dive in. Her body jolts as if struck by an electrical current when I flatten my tongue and lick her repeatedly.

Her moaning and grinding have me going ape-shit. My body begs for release, just as hers is doing against my mouth. Ladies first, right?

I lap at her as I run both of my hands up her body, spreading her open. Revealing the most sensitive part of her body, I suck her clit into my mouth, softly at first then increasing suction. She's trembling, begging me for more, and asking me to stop as her body tries to handle all the sensations at once.

I sink two, strong fingers inside of her and nearly come as her body receives the attention and begins convulsing and clenching at me. The pulse against my tongue has my own cock weeping. I'm unable to wait another second even though her orgasm is still in full effect.

I stand abruptly and pull her to her feet.

"Legs around my waist," I insist as I lift her under my arms.

Like a homing beacon that knows exactly where it's heading, my cock stands up straight and seeks her heat as I lower her down my shaft.

I growl as her nails bite into the back of my neck, her lips quivering with a soft whimper.

"You okay?" I ask as I lift her slightly then lower her back down.

She nods her head slightly and lowers her mouth to mine. I take her in a heated kiss unlike any other we've shared. Needing the leverage, I walk us to the wall and place her gently against it, even though I feel like nothing short of a feral animal at this point.

"Wasn't planning on fucking you against a wall tonight," I admit against her neck.

She circles her hips, grinding down harder. "I love it when you're out of control."

I nip at her neck in response. Gripping under both ass cheeks, I flex my hips back and slide back in. My rhythm picks up, her moans and whimpers matching the tempo of my thrusting hips. I'd love nothing more than to last all night with this incredible woman, but even sixty more seconds seems like a battle I'm going to lose.

"Rub your clit," I beg. "I need you to come again."

She moans loudly in my ear as I feel her hand pull from my neck and slide down between us. I shift her weight and pull my torso back so I can see our joining and her tiny hand toying with her clit.

We lock eyes just before she tugs my head, placing her forehead against mine. Our harsh pants of breath mix, and the tightening of her core gives me permission to let go. Never taking our eyes from one another, I groan as my body gives into hers and my climax meets a spectacular high. I pulse inside of her as she clamps down on me in long grasps.

I continue to slide her up and down me until our pulses begin to slow and our breaths even out.

I kiss her chin softly and carry her to the bathroom for a much-needed shower.

Chapter 33
Aviana

Waking up in the arms of a naked BT could easily become one of my favorite things to do. I snuggle deeper into his embrace and run my fingers over the light smattering of hair on his abdomen. He tightens his arm around my waist, and I smile against his chest.

I'm overcome with emotion. The past few weeks have been hell on both of us. I'm feeling and thinking things I've never let my mind wander to in the past. I want a future, I want BT, and for the first time since my dad walked away from me and my mom, I want to share my life with a man.

He told me on the plane yesterday that he loved me and my heart nearly stopped. It's not the first time I've heard the words from a man's mouth, but it's most definitely the first time they've been spoken, and I could feel the truth in them. I was so wrapped up in him I didn't say the words back, and by the time I could finally admit to myself I felt the same way, the moment had already passed.

I refuse to let another second go by where he could be wondering where we stand. I don't know exactly what happens when we get back to Tampa, but he's promised me there's an *us*, so I take the leap, jumping off a cliff I've never interacted with before in my life.

"I love you, too," I say softly against the bare skin of his chest, hoping it was loud enough for him to hear.

His body freezes, but his heart begins to thunder loudly in his chest. I swallow roughly waiting for his reaction.

Slowly he pulls himself out from under me and eases me to my back.

"Avi," he says reverently against my parted lips.

I close my eyes as his hand reaches up and runs down my cheek and jawline. He shifts his weight between my thighs and I open myself up to him, both physically and figuratively.

"Say it again," he pleads as I feel him slide against my already wet center.

"I love you," I say on a moan as he pushes slowly inside of me.

Without another word from our lips, we allow our bodies to speak all of the truths of our hearts.

***

BT's mood has changed since we made love this morning, and his saddened demeanor has my nerves set on edge. I'm worried after giving my heart away he's about to crush me.

He's attentive in the shower, never taking his hands from my body, but he's not smiled since we got in here. His face is always marked with a smile, and even though it's only been a few minutes, I'm missing his dimples dearly.

"Baby, we need to talk," he whispers looking down at me as the water cascades over our bodies. I can see regret in his eyes, and I close my eyes waiting for the pain.

I nod, knowing his words are going to slay me.

"I told you your dad was at your apartment when I went looking for you." I look up at him, not expecting things to go this direction.

"He had so many drugs running through his system, half of the things he said made no sense. I got the info I needed and left. At that point, you were my only concern." He lowers his head and sighs. "The guys from the club went to Tampa looking for more information than I was able to get in the short period of time I had searched for your whereabouts."

I place a calming hand on his chest, hating his pain even though I know mine is still coming.

"When the guys got to your place, your dad was still there."

I wait for him to tell me that he's destroyed all of my belongings or moved a gaggle of homeless people into my apartment.

"Your dad," he says and pauses shaking his head slightly. "They found your dad deceased on the couch."

I gasp and take a step back. Tears I never thought would fall again for the man who deserted me years ago begin to fall down my already wet cheeks.

"What happened to him?" I know it was a shitty neighborhood, and every second I was there, I felt like I was in danger.

"He overdosed. Shadow told me they called the police and had the body recovered. I don't know anything past that."

My heart is hammering in my ears, and a wave of guilt washes over me when I feel relieved that his sadness has nothing to do with him leaving or not wanting me when we get back to Florida.

Don't get me wrong; I'm sad about the news of my dad, but I always knew in the back of my mind that this is what would happen to him. Last time I saw him, he looked near death's door. I begged and pleaded with him to get help, but he insisted he didn't have a problem, even though the sores on his skin and track marks all over his arms told a different story.

We finish our shower and dress in silence. There are so many things we have to face once we get back home, the idea of it all is exhausting. I'd love to do nothing more than climb in the bed and have him hold me, but that's not on the agenda today. Today we return to a city that has no meaning to me any longer. The only bright side is BT and the promises he's made me.

"Let's go get breakfast," he says offering his hand to me.

I'm numb with regret and words unspoken for a man I never really knew. Knowing I'll never be able to confront him for twenty plus years of wrong doing sits heavy in my stomach.

Walking into the kitchen for breakfast, I notice two things at once. One, the women seemed to have found most of their clothes overnight, a fact I'm grateful for. I was very uneasy last night knowing BT was in a room of half-naked women, even though he didn't show one hint of interest in them. Two, Darby is sitting in Snatch's lap like she's known him all her life.

I smile at her as we make our way to the buffet of food on the counter. The room is full of members wearing leather vests and women chatting. The noise and interaction are refreshing since I'd been all but solitary for the last couple of weeks.

We load up our plates and head over to a nearly empty table across the room. A very young, clearly sullen girl looks up from the cup of coffee she's staring in as if it holds all the answers in life. I give her a gentle smile because not long ago I had that same look on my face.

"Hi," I say placing my plate on the table. "I'm Aviana," I smile at BT as he settles in beside me.

"Khloe," she says. I see her peer across the room before she gets up, leaving her still full coffee on the table.

I raise my eyes and look in the direction she'd just stared in finding a young biker, staring at her retreating back. He looks sadden by her departure but doesn't make a move to follow her out of the room. Trouble in paradise it seems. He looks my direction, nodding his head in acknowledgment. I lower my eyes immediately, embarrassed to have been caught staring at him. I don't know their story and probably never will, but the tension between the two could easily be cut with a knife.

I feel a presence beside me and lift my eyes to see Darby settling in Khloe's vacant seat.

"We're heading out in an hour or so," BT says from my other side.

I look back to Darby. "You going to be ready to go?"

She looks over in the direction I know Snatch is sitting in. "Change of plans," she says with a smile from ear to ear. "I think I'm going to stay here for a bit."

I raise both my eyebrows at her, but she's watching him across the room, paying me no mind. I look over and see Snatch sitting leaned back deep in his chair with a satisfied look on his face.

"Do you think that's the best idea?" I ask her, having no idea what this MC is like. They seem like nice people, but without interacting with them, I honestly have no idea.

"She's welcome to stay as long as she likes," I hear from across the table. Kincaid, as he was introduced to me last night, has sat down with a beautiful blonde while I was distracted by Darby. The woman beside him is absolutely beautiful, and she doesn't seem to have a problem with another woman joining the group.

"Emmalyn," she says holding her hand out to me. I shake it with a smile. Not exactly the type of woman you'd expect to see in the middle of a motorcycle club, but I'm quickly learning my perceptions, mainly reinforced by too many episodes of SOA, are clearly wrong.

"You sure?" I ask Darby again.

"Absolutely," she answers. Kissing me on the cheek, she stands from the table and returns to the waiting, tattooed arms of the scariest biker in this place.

***

The plane ride back to Tampa is spent in silence. I had a million questions last night, and those have only seemed to double after the news of my father's death. As we draw closer to Florida, they've taken over completely.

I turn slightly in my seat and look at BT only to find him watching me. He smiles at me and holds the hand in my lap tighter. My abduction and rescue have taken over his life, and I'm grateful for him dropping his life back home and coming to find me. This is also the reason I'm unsure about how much my life is going to be tangled with his.

I drop my eyes to my hands, unable to formulate the questions I have into actual sentences.

He tilts my chin back up, forcing me to look into his eyes.

"Come home with me," he whispers as if he can read my mind and all the doubts I have about returning to Florida.

"I may never want to leave again," I counter.

"That's my hope," he says before his mouth crashes against mine, almost indecently considering we're in the middle of a commercial plane.

Epilogue
Aviana

My incredible luck, since BT came into my life, thankfully, hasn't run out.

Returning home and having to plan a small memorial for my father was tough, but manageable with BT by my side. I never returned to the acting studio, deciding I was no longer going to waste my life or time on things that had no future. With BT's help, I was able to get into the University of Tampa, focusing on counseling. Sports medicine seemed like a good idea, but I realized that helping people heal from the inside out is going to be more rewarding for me than helping with sports injuries and such.

BT has continued to work as a personal trainer, but he too stopped the acting classes. He's had several more offers for book covers and has photo shoots scheduled with several well-known photographers, including one with the incredible Christopher John next month. I found out after moving in with him that he has a worldwide fan base of women and men alike. That took some getting used to, but he's never given me any reason to doubt his loyalty to me and our growing relationship.

Walking into the house that seamlessly became my home after returning from Vegas, I hang my purse in the hall closet and seek out my other half.

I catch him carrying a large covered dish from the kitchen to the dining room table. He stops in his tracks when he notices me standing in the doorway.

"You're home early," he says somewhat guiltily.

I narrow my eyes at him. "Just what kind of trouble are you getting into, Mr. Urruela," I ask taking in the perfect place settings at the table and the tall candles waiting to be lit.

He grins from ear to ear. "Spaghetti. If memory serves, you love it."

"No garlic bread?" I tease.

"Not a fucking chance," he says. "Have a seat, baby. Let me grab the wine."

I sit down to the table and wonder just what he has up his sleeves. Most days we make a quick dinner together then hang out in the living room, chatting quietly while we eat. It's Tuesday, which is a weird day for a romantic dinner for two, but I'm not going to snub my nose at it, that's for sure.

BT carries the wine to the table but leans in for a kiss before pulling away and leaving me breathless. This man is absolute perfection. I never wake up in the morning or leave the house for work or school and not feel every ounce of his love.

He pours us each a glass of burgundy wine and takes a seat beside me. I just watch him as he dishes out delicious smelling spaghetti. It's not exactly a gourmet meal, but it's very us.

He winks at me as he places the serving spoon back in the dish and picks up his own fork.

I mimic his actions, but can't seem to concentrate enough to eat. He seems to be struggling due to the smile across his face.

"What's going on?" I ask reaching for my glass of wine.

"Do you remember the first time we had spaghetti at this table?" I nod. "That was six months ago."

"Are you the type of guy who celebrates half year anniversaries?" I ask with a smirk.

"Clearly," he says and waves his hand as if showcasing the spread before us.

"I love that about you," I admit.

"I love *you*," he says placing his fork down on his plate.

I watch him straighten his leg and pull a small box from his pocket. My heart sputters and then beats wildly in my chest. We've promised each other forever. We say it often, but I never expected this.

"I got you something," he says placing the black velvet box beside my plate. "Open it," he insists when my hand stutters to a stop on the top of it without picking it up.

Slowly, I pull the box from the table and pop open the lid. Just as I'm about to scream 'YES' I see a beautiful set of pink diamond earrings in my hand. I swallow roughly, trying to shove down the disappointment and give this man the thanks he deserves for such a beautiful gift.

I'm unable to catch the tear that threads its way down my cheek.

"Thank you," I finally manage to look up at him. "They're beautiful."

"You seem..." he pauses, "disappointed."

I shake my head no, lying to him for the first time in our relationship.

I feel him move closer, but do my best to school my face before looking at him again.

"Maybe this will help?" he asks.

I look up and find him kneeling in front of me, displaying the most amazing diamond ring I've ever seen.

"You asshole," I say through sobs of happiness.

"Is that a yes?"

I nod my head feverishly and jump into his arms, knocking us both to the floor.

Acknowledgments

This usually the hardest part of the book to write (well, other than that damn blurb.)

This go around for some reason seems so easy. There are so many people to thank, so many generous people who've helped to make this book a reality.

First and foremost, extreme recognition goes to the man of the hour, BT Urruela. One simple post on another model's page forced me into action. BT requested a FanFiction of his own, and I knew I had to be the one to oblige. BT is the epitome of humble sacrifice. He's sacrificed so much for his country, his fans, and I'm willing to bet he's nowhere near done yet.

When speaking with BT about this book, his direction was 'complete chaos', but then of course followed that up with "but nothing too crazy." This book may be the only Marie James books he's read, and I'm certain after reading it, he's wishing he had given more specific directions. Nonetheless, he's given me the go ahead to publish, which I'm forever grateful. There are hints of BT's life throughout the book, as any fan who stalks himself regularly will be able to pick out with ease. If at any point in the book, you questioned whether or not the character was displaying 'odd for BT' traits, that's all on me. Please keep in mind it is a FanFiction, meaning not much of it is real.

Secondly, I want to thank Christopher John for donating the fabulous picture on the cover. He didn't hesitate once when I explained exactly what I was doing for the book. He's checked up regularly on the progress as it was written and is genuinely excited about reading it.

The wonderful Kari Ayasha did the magnificent cover design and also donated her services. She's created each and every one of my covers, and I remain humbled by her talent.

Give Me Books also donated their time and skills for the promotional part of making sure SINdicate reached as many people as it could. They have been wonderful to work with on promotions for most of my books. Any author seeking a wide audience should consider using them.

I want to thank my husband, Author JA Essen for always believing in me, supporting me with my crazy writing, and for always being the one I feel comfortable bouncing ideas off of. He also helped with editing on SINdicate and I always value his skills and attention to detail.

I would get absolutely nowhere without my BETA team. Brittney, Brenda, Shannon, Diane, Amanda, Charlie, Tammy, Jessica, and Kendra are vital to the success of my books. They keep me grounded when I need, and sometimes even ride my ass when I'm not getting things done fast enough. They helped with inspiration for SINdicate by posting some of the most phenomenal pictures of BT in our private group, but seriously have we ever seen a non-phenomenal picture of BT? I haven't seen one yet I don't love!

Brittney Crabtree... What can I say about my main bitch to even give her half as much credit as she deserves? She's my rock in this crazy Indie world. She's talked me off the ledge more than once, and I know I can trust her to not blow smoke up my ass. If something isn't working or if my attitude gets out of hand, she's always there to give me the kick in the ass I need. Numerous phone calls, hours of plotting and opinions on not just this book but several of my last ones have been provided without so much as one complaint. She's invaluable to literary empire I'm working desperately to build! Love you sKunt.

To all my fans, without you none of this would even be possible. I never imagined a year ago when I sat down to write the first sentence in Coming to Hale did I ever imagine that there would someone out there who would even want to read it. My fan base is comprised of some of the best women (and a couple of FanBoys) I could ever be associated with. Thanks for coming along this wonderful ride with me!!

Side note If there are any grammatical errors in this section, blame me. My BETAs don't get to proof read this section of the book until it goes live.

More from Marie James

Marie James Facebook: Marie James
Author Group: Author Marie James All Hale Fans
Twitter: @AuthrMarieJame
Instagram: author_marie_james

Hale Series
Coming to Hale
Begging for Hale
Hot as Hale
To Hale and Back
Hale Series Box Set

Love Me Like That

Cerberus MC
Kincaid

Kid

(Kid releases June 22nd)

Psychosis
Matthew Hosea FanFiction Novella
Co-write with Gina Sevani

Printed in Great Britain
by Amazon